MERCIER IRISH CLASSICS
Traits & Stories of the Irish Peasantry, Volume IV

THE PARTY FIGHT AND FUNERAL

by

WILLIAM CARLETON

With an Introduction by
MAURICE HARMON

THE MERCIER PRESS
Cork and Dublin

THE MERCIER PRESS LIMITED
4 Bridge Street, Cork
25 Lower Abbey Street, Dublin 1

THE PARTY FIGHT AND FUNERAL

ISBN 0 85342 342 3

Introduction © Maurice Harmon 1973

This is Volume 4 of a series of eight volumes containing a complete and unabridged edition of William Carleton's *Traits & Stories of the Irish Peasantry*

Printed in Ireland by
the Leinster Leader Limited

CONTENTS

INTRODUCTION TO VOLUME FOUR

THE two long stories in this volume are related in subject matter in that each sets out to illustrate the evils of Ribbonism, and of sectarianism, in Irish society. Carleton had experienced the consequences of sectarian bitterness in that childhood scene when local Orangemen beat at his father's door and pushed their way into the house in search of arms. He was himself a member of the Ribbon society, knew its secret signs and oaths, and its conspiratorial hold on the people. He knew too the prominent part played in it by the local teacher who was generally master also of the local Ribbon lodge. He had seen too what happened to twenty-four "brothers" in County Louth after the burning out of the Lynch family in Wildgoose Lodge when he came across their rotting bodies hanging from gibbets. He also saw the violence of the faction fights about which he also wrote a story in which his old teacher Pat Frayne remembers his fights with the O'Hallaghans.

These fights, like those of the Montagues and Capulets, have no known original cause and seem destined to go on endlessly. Wives, mothers, and moderate men, as "The Party Fight and Funeral" is careful to show, cry out for a cessation to the endemic violence that causes so much suffering and death, but little boys at school mimic the madness of the adults and even succeed in planning their battles on the same day their fathers clash. There is the telling scene in this story in which the boy swears to take vengeance for his father's death: "Oh! the murdherers, oh! the murderers, the murdherers!" he exclaimed, "that killed my father; for only for them, he would be still wid us: but, by the God that's over me, if I live, night or day I will not rest, till I have blood for blood; nor do I care who hears it, nor if I was hanged the next minute." In an ominous note Carleton says "Such were the words". Even more frightening is the surge of emotional vengeance that sweeps through the boy's relations as they repeat "almost word for word, the vow of vengeance which the son had just sworn." And so the pattern of violence, death and reprisal repeats itself. Carleton's didacticism gets in the way of his story, but it is nevertheless a powerful illumination of the evil of Ribbonism and has many memorable scenes, such as the reckless approach of the attackers on Vesey's house, the gladiatorial combat of the two leaders—like something out of an Irish saga— the bearing of the body to the door of the "murdered" and the curse of the widow.

One remarkable feature of the story is the sense of life in the locality. Four to five thousand people line up on opposing sides for the battle. The same feeling runs all through "The Midnight Mass", of a populated countryside with its own distinctive culture and traditions. This Gothic story builds a complex, interrelated world of religious commemoration, dancing, jealous quarreling, a planned abduction leading to murder, and deeper still, permeating the whole society, the hidden power of the Ribbonmen. It was in fact during a dance that Carleton had been given the oath that made him a member of this organisation: "What age are we in? The end of the fifth. What's the hour? Very near the right one. Isn't it come yet? The hour is come, but not the man. When will he come? He is within sight." In time he would produce it in the story "Tubber Derg" and would in his second novel *Rody the Rover* attack the peasant organisation that had been created to fight the landlords.

THE PARTY FIGHT AND FUNERAL [1]

IT has long been laid down as a universal principle that self-preservation is the first law of nature. An Irishman, however, has nothing to do with this; he disposes of it as he does of the other laws, and washes his hands out of it altogether. But commend him to a fair, dance, funeral, or wedding, or to any other sport where there is a likelihood of getting his head or his bones broken, and if he survive he will remember you, with a kindness peculiar to himself, to the last day of his life; will drub you from head to heel if he finds that any misfortune has kept you out of a row beyond the usual period of three months; will render the same service to any of your friends that stand in need of it; or, in short, will go to the world's end, or fifty miles farther, as he himself would say, to serve you, provided you can procure him a bit of decent fighting. Now, in truth and soberness, it is difficult to account for this propensity, especially when the task of ascertaining it is assigned to those of another country, or even to those Irishmen whose rank in life places them too far from the customs, prejudices, and domestic opinions of their native peasantry—none of which can be properly known without mingling with them. To my own knowledge, however, it proceeds from education. And here I would beg leave to point out an omission of which the several boards of education have been guilty, and which, I believe, no one but myself has yet been sufficiently acute and philosophical to ascertain, as forming a *sine quâ non* in the national instruction of the lower orders of Irishmen.

---

[1] We ought, perhaps, to inform our readers that the connection between a party fight and funeral is sufficiently strong to justify the author in classing them under the title which is prefixed to this story. The one, being usually the natural result of the other, is made to proceed from it, as is the custom in real life among the Irish.

The cream of the matter is this. A species of ambition prevails in the Green Isle not known in any other country. It is an ambition of about three miles by four in extent—or, in other words, is bounded by the limits of the parish in which the subject of it may reside. It puts itself forth early in the character, and a hardy perennial it is. In my own case its first development was noticed in the hedge-school which I attended. I had not been long there till I was forced to declare myself either for the Caseys or the Murphys, two tiny factions that had split the school between them. The day on which the ceremony of my declaration took place was a solemn one. After school, we all went to the bottom of a deep valley, a short distance from the schoolhouse. Up to the moment of our assembling there, I had not taken my stand under either banner—that of the Caseys was a sod of turf stuck on the end of a broken fishing-rod; the eagle of the Murphys was a cork-red potato hoisted in the same manner. The turf was borne by an urchin who afterwards distinguished himself at fairs and markets as a *builla battha* of the first grade, and from this circumstance he was nick-named *Parrah Rackhan*.[1] The potato was borne by little Mickle M'Phaudeen Murphy, who afterwards took away Katty Bane Sheridan without asking her own consent or her father's. They were all then boys, it is true, but they gave a tolerable promise of that eminence which they subsequently attained.

When we arrived at the bottom of the glen, the Murphys and the Caseys, including their respective followers, ranged themselves on either side of a long line which was drawn between the belligerent powers with the butt-end of one of the standards. Exactly on this line was I placed. The word was then put to me in full form—"Whether will you side with the dacent Caseys or the blackguard Murphys?" "Whether will you side with the dacent Murphys or the blackguard Caseys?" "The potato for ever!" said I, throwing up my *caubeen*, and running over to the Murphy standard. In the twinkling of an eye we were at it; and in a short time the deuce an eye some of us had to twinkle.

[1] Paddy Riot (or the Rioter).

2

A battle-royal succeeded that lasted near half an hour, and it would probably have lasted about double the time were it not for the appearance of the "master," who was seen by a little shrivelled *vidette*, who wanted an arm, and could take no part in the engagement. This was enough; we instantly radiated in all possible directions, so that by the time he had descended through the intricacies of the glen to the field of battle neither victor nor vanquished was visible, except, perhaps, a straggler or two as they topped the brow of the declivity, looking back over their shoulders to put themselves out of doubt as to their visibility by the master. They seldom looked in vain, however; for there he usually stood, shaking up his rod, silently prophetic of its application on the following day. This threat, for the most part, ended in smoke; for, except he horsed about forty or fifty of us, the infliction of impartial justice was utterly out of his power.

But, besides this, there never was a realm in which the evils of a divided cabinet were more visible: the truth is, the monarch himself was under the influence of female government—an influence which he felt it either contrary to his inclination or beyond his power to throw off. "Poor Norah, long may you reign," we often used to exclaim, to the visible mortification of the "master," who felt the benevolence of the wish bottomed upon an indirect want of allegiance to himself. Well, it was a touching scene— how we used to stand with the waistbands of our small-clothes cautiously grasped in our hands, with a timid show of resistance, our brave red faces slobbered over with tears, as we stood naked for execution! Never was there a finer specimen of deprecation in eloquence than we then exhibited —the supplicating look right up into the master's face; the touching modulation of the whine; the additional tightness and caution with which we grasped the waistbands with one hand, when it was necessary to use the other in wiping our eyes and noses with the polished sleeve-cuff; the sincerity and vehemence with which we promised never to be guilty again, still shrewdly including the condition of present impunity for our offence: "this—one—time—master, if ye plaise, sir;" and the utter hopelessness and despair which

3

were legible in the last groan, as we grasped the "master's" leg in utter recklessness of judgment, were all perfect in their way. Reader, have you ever got a reprieve from the gallows? I beg pardon, my dear sir; I only meant to ask, are you capable of entering into what a personage of that description might be supposed to feel, on being informed, after the knot had been neatly tied under the left ear, and the cap drawn over his eyes, that his Majesty had granted him a full pardon? But you remember your own schoolboy days, and that's enough.

The nice discrimination with which Norah used to time her interference was indeed surprising. God help us! limited was our experience, and shallow our little judgments, or we might, with less trouble than Sir Humphry Davy deciphered the Herculaneum MSS., have known what the master meant when, with the uplifted arm hung over us, his eye was fixed upon the door of the kitchen, waiting for Norah's appearance.

Long, my fair and virtuous countrywomen—I repeat it to you all, as I did to Norah—may you reign in the hearts and affections of your husbands (but nowhere else), the grace, ornaments, and happiness of their hearths and lives, you jewels, you! You are paragons of all that's good, and your feelings are highly creditable to yourselves and to humanity.

When Norah advanced, with her brawny uplifted arm (for she was a powerful woman) and forbidding aspect, to interpose between us and the avenging terrors of the birch, do you think that she did not reflect honour on her sex and the national character? I sink the base allusion to the *miscaun* of fresh butter which we had placed in her hands that morning, or the dish of eggs or of meal which we had either begged or stolen at home, as a present for her; disclaiming, at the same time, the rascally idea of giving it from any motive beneath the most lofty-minded and disinterested generosity on our part.

Then, again, never did a forbidding face shine with so winning and amicable an expression as did hers on that merciful occasion. The sun dancing a hornpipe on Easter Sunday morning, or the full moon sailing as proud as a peacock in a new halo head-dress, was a very disrespectable

4

sight compared to Norah's red, beaming face, shrouded in her dowd cap with long ears that descended to her masculine and substantial neck. Owing to her influence, the whole economy of the school was good; for we were permitted to cuff one another, and do whatever we please, with impunity, if we brought the meal, eggs, or butter; except some scape-goat who was not able to accomplish this, and he generally received on his own miserable carcase what was due to us all.

Poor Jack Murray! his last words on the scaffold, for being concerned in the murder of Pierce the gauger, were, that he got the first of his bad habits under Pat Mulligan and Norah—that he learned to steal by secreting at home butter and meal to paste up the master's eyes to his bad conduct—and that his fondness for quarrelling arose from being per-mitted to head a faction at school; a most ungrateful return for the many acts of grace which the indulgence of Norah caused to be issued in his favour.

I was but a short time under Pat, when, after the general example, I had my cudgel, which I used to carry regularly to a certain furze bush within fifty perches of the "seminary," where I hid it till after "dismiss." I grant it does not look well in me to become my own panegyrist; but I can at least declare that there were few among the Caseys able to resist the prowess of this right arm, puny as it was at the period in question. Our battles were obstinate and frequent; but as the quarrels of the two families and their relations on each side were as bitter and pugnacious in fairs and markets as ours were in school, we hit upon the plan of holding our Lilliputian engagements upon the same days on which our fathers and brothers contested. According to this plan, it very often happened that the corresponding parties were successful, and as frequently that whilst the Caseys were well drubbed in the fair, their sons were victorious at school, and *vice versâ*.

For my part I was early trained to cudgelling, and before I reached my fourteenth year could pronounce as sage and accurate an opinion upon the merits of a *shillelagh*, as it is called, or cudgel, as a veterinary surgeon of sixty could upon a dead ass at first sight. Our plan of preparing is this. We sallied out to any place where there was an underwood of blackthorn or oak, and having surveyed the premises with the eye of a connoisseur, we selected the straightest root-growing piece which we could find; for if not root-growing, we did not consider it worth cutting, knowing from experience that a branch, how straight and fair soever it might look, would snap in the twist and tug of war. Having cut it as close to the root as possible, we then lopped off the branches, and put it up in the chimney to season. When seasoned, we took it down, and wrapping it in brown paper, well steeped in hog's lard or oil, we buried it in a horse-dunghill, paying it a daily visit for the purpose of making it straight by doubling back the bends or angles across the knee, in a direction contrary to their natural tendency. Having daily repeated this until we had made it straight, and renewed the oiled wrapping-paper until the staff was perfectly saturated, we then rubbed it well with a woollen cloth containing a little black-lead and grease, to give it a polish. This was the last process; except that if we thought it too light at the top, we used to bore a hole in the lower end with a red-hot iron spindle, into which we poured melted lead, for the purpose of giving it the knock-down weight.

There were very few of Paddy Mulligan's scholars without a choice collection of them, and scarcely one who had not, before his fifteenth year, a just claim to be called the hero of a hundred fights, and the heritor of as many bumps on the cranium as would strike both Gall and Spurzheim speechless.

Now this, be it known, was, and in some districts yet is, an integral part of an Irish peasant's education. In the northern parts of Ireland, where the population of the Catholics on the one side, and of Protestants and Dissenters on the other, is nearly equal, I have known the respective scholars of Catholic and Protestant schools to challenge each other, and meet half-way to do battle, in vindication of their respective creeds; or for the purpose of establishing the character of their respective masters as the more learned man; for if we were to judge by the nature of the education then received, we would be led to conclude that a more commercial nation than Ireland was not on the face of the earth, it being the indispensable part of every scholar's

6

business to become acquainted with the three sets of book-keeping.

The boy who was the handiest and the most daring with the cudgel at Paddy Mulligan's school was Denis Kelly, the son of a wealthy farmer in the neighbourhood. He was a rash, hot-tempered, good-natured lad, possessing a more than common share of this blackthorn ambition; on which account he was cherished by his relations as a boy that was likely at a future period to be able to walk over the course of the parish in fair, market, or patron. He certainly grew up a stout, able young fellow, and before he reached nineteen years was un-rivalled at the popular exercises of the peasantry. Shortly after that time he made his *début* in a party quarrel, which took place in one of the Christmas *maragah-mores*, and fully sustained the anticipations which were formed of him by his relations. For a year or two afterwards no quarrel was fought without him; and his prowess rose until he had gained the very pinnacle of that ambition which he had determined to reach. About this time I was separated from him, having found it necessaay, in order to accomplish my objects in life, to reside with a relation in another part of the country.

The period of my absence, I believe, was about fourteen years, during which space I heard no account of him what-soever. At length, however, that inextinguishable attach-ment which turns the affections and memory to the friends of our early days—to those scenes which we traversed when the heart was light and the spirits buoyant—determined me to make a visit to my native place, that I might witness the progress of time and care upon those faces that were once so familiar to me; that I might once more look upon the meadows, and valleys, and groves, and mountains where I had so often played, and to which I still found myself bound by a tie that a more enlightened view of life and nature only made stronger and more enduring. I accordingly set off, and arrived, late in the evening of a December day, at a little town within a few miles of my native home. On alighting from the coach, and dining, I determined to walk home, as it was a fine frosty night. The full moon hung in the blue unclouded firmament in all her lustre, and the stars shone

7

out with that tremulous twinkling motion so peculiarly remarkable in frost. I had been absent, I said, about fourteen years, and felt that the enjoyment of this night would form an era in the records of my memory and my feelings. I find myself, indeed, utterly incapable of expressing what I experienced; but those who have ever been in similar circumstances will understand what I mean. A strong spirit of practical poetry and romance was upon me, and I thought that a commonplace approach in the open day would have rendered my return to the scenes of my early life a very stale and unedifying matter.

I left the inn at seven o'clock, and as I had only five miles to walk, I would just arrive about nine, allowing myself to saunter on at the rate of two miles and a half per hour. My sensations, indeed, as I went along, were singular; and as I took a solitary road across the mountains, the loneliness of the walk, the deep gloom of the valleys, the towering height of the dark hills, and the pale silvery light of a sleeping lake shining dimly in the distance below, gave me such a distinct notion of the sublime and beautiful as I have seldom since experienced. I recommend every man who has been fourteen years absent from his native fields to return by moonlight.

Well, there is a mystery yet undiscovered in our being, for no man can know his feelings or his capacities. Many a slumbering thought, and sentiment, and association reposes within him of which he is utterly ignorant, and which, except he come in contact with those objects whose influence over his mind can alone call them into being, may never be awakened, or give him one moment of either pleasure or pain. There is, therefore, a great deal in the position which we hold in society, and simply in situation. I felt this on that night; for the tenor of my reflections was new and original, and my feelings had a warmth and freshness in them which nothing but the situation in which I then found myself could give them. The force of association, too, was powerful; for, as I advanced nearer home, the names of hills, and lakes, and mountains that I had utterly forgotten, as I thought, were distinctly revived in my memory, and a crowd of youthful thoughts and feelings that I imagined my intercourse with the world and the finger of time had blotted out of my being

8

began to crowd afresh on my fancy. The name of a townland would instantly return with its appearance; and I could now remember the history of families and individuals that had long been effaced from my recollection.

But what is even more singular is that the superstitious terrors of my boyhood began to come over me, as formerly, whenever a spot noted for supernatural appearances met my eye. It was in vain that I exerted myself to expel them, by throwing the barrier of philosophic reasoning in their way; they still clung to me, in spite of every effort to the contrary. But the fact is that I was for the moment the slave of a morbid and feverish sentiment, that left me completely at the mercy of the dark and fleeting images that passed over my fancy. I now came to a turn where the road began to slope down into the depths of a valley that ran across it. When I looked forward into the bottom, all was darkness impenetrable, for the moonbeams were thrown off by the height of the mountains that rose on each side of it. I felt an indefinite sensation of fear, because at that moment I recollected that it had been, in my younger days, notorious as the scene of an apparition, where the spirit of a murdered pedlar had never been known to permit a solitary traveller to pass without appearing to him, and walking cheek-by-jowl along with him to the next house on the way, at which spot he usually vanished. The influence of my feelings, or, I should rather say, the physical excitement of my nerves, was by no means slight as these old traditions recurred to me; although, at the same time, my moral courage was perfectly unimpaired, so that, notwithstanding this involuntary apprehension, I felt a degree of novelty and curiosity in descending the valley. "If it appear," said I, "I shall at least satisfy myself as to the truth of apparitions."

My dress consisted of a long dark surtout, the collar of which, as the night was keen, I had turned up about my ears, and the corners of it met round my face. In addition to this I had a black silk handkerchief tied across my mouth to keep out the night air; so that, as my dark fur travelling cap came down over my face, there was very little of my countenance visible. I now had advanced half-way into the valley, and all about me was dark and still: the moonlight

9

was not nearer than the top of the hill which I was descending; and I often turned round to look upon it, so silvery and beautiful it appeared at a distance. Sometimes I stood for a few moments admiring its effect, and contemplating the dark mountains as they stood out against the firmament, then kindled into magnificent grandeur by the myriads of stars that glowed in its expanse. There was perfect silence and solitude around me; and as I stood alone in the dark chamber of the mountains I felt the impressiveness of the situation gradually supersede my terrors. A sublime sense of religious awe descended on me; my soul kindled into a glow of solemn and elevated devotion, which gave me a more intense perception of the presence of God than I had ever before experienced. "How sacred—how awful," thought I, "is this place!—how impressive is this hour!—surely I feel myself at the footstool of God! The voice of worship is in this deep, soul-thrilling silence; and the tongue of praise speaks, as it were, from the very solitude of the mountains!" I then thought of Him who went up into a mountain-top to pray, and felt the majesty of those admirable descriptions of the Almighty given in the Old Testament blend in delightful harmony with the beauty and fitness of the Christian dispensation, that brought life and immortality to light. "Here," said I, "do I feel that I am indeed immortal, and destined for scenes of a more exalted and comprehensive existence!"

I then proceeded farther into the valley, completely freed from the influence of old and superstitious associations. A few perches below me a small river crossed the road, over which was thrown a little stone bridge of rude workmanship. This bridge was the spot on which the apparition was said to appear; and as I approached it I felt the folly of those terrors which had only a few minutes before beset me so strongly. I found my moral energies recruited, and the dark phantasms of my imagination dispelled by the light of religion, which had refreshed me with a deep sense of the Almighty presence. I accordingly walked forward, scarcely bestowing a thought upon the history of the place, and had got within a few yards of the bridge, when, on resting my eye accidentally upon the little elevation formed by its rude arch, I perceived a black

10

coffin placed at the edge of the road, exactly upon the bridge!

It may be evident to the reader that, however satisfactory the force of philosophical reasoning might have been upon the subject of the solitude, I was too much the creature of sensation for an hour before to look on such a startling object with firm nerves. For the first two or three minutes, therefore, I exhibited as finished a specimen of the dastardly as could be imagined. My hair absolutely raised my cap some inches off my head; my mouth opened to an extent which I did not conceive it could possibly reach; I thought my eyes shot out from their sockets; and my fingers spread out and became stiff, though powerless. The *obstupui* was perfectly realised in me; for, with the exception of a single groan which I gave on first seeing the object, I found that if one word would save my life or transport me to my own fireside, I could not utter it. I was also rooted to the earth as if by magic; and although instant tergiversation and flight had my most hearty concurrence, I could not move a limb, nor even raise my eye off the sepulchral-looking object which lay before me. I now felt the perspiration fall from my face in torrents, and the strokes of my heart fell audibly on my ear. I even attempted to say, "God preserve me," but my tongue was dumb and powerless, and could not move. My eye was still upon the coffin, when I perceived that, from being motionless, it instantly began to swing, first in a lateral, then in a longitudinal direction, although it was perfectly evident that no human hand was nearer it than my own. At length I raised my eyes off it, for my vision was strained to an aching intensity which I thought must have occasioned my eye-strings to crack. I looked instinctively. about me for assistance—but all was dismal, silent, and solitary; even the moon had disappeared among a few clouds that I had not noticed in the sky.

As I stood in this state of indescribable horror I saw the light gradually fade away from the tops of the mountains, giving the scene around me a dim and spectral ghastliness, which to those who were never in such a situation is altogether inconceivable.

At length I thought I heard a noise as it were of a rushing

11

tempest sweeping from the hills down into the valley; but on looking up I could perceive nothing but the dusky desolation that brooded over the place. Still the noise continued; again I saw the coffin move; I then felt the motion communicated to myself, and found my body borne and swung backwards and forwards, precisely according to the motion of the coffin. I again attempted to utter a cry for assistance, but could not. The motion of my body still continued, as did the approaching noise in the hills. I looked up a second time in the direction in which the valley wound off between them, but judge of what I must have suffered when I beheld one of the mountains moving, as it were, from its base, and tumbling down towards the spot on which I stood. In the twinkling of an eye the whole scene, hills and all, began to tremble, to vibrate and to fly round me with a rapid, delirious motion; the stars shot back into the depths of heaven, and disappeared; the ground on which I stood began to pass from beneath my feet; a noise like the breaking of a thousand gigantic billows again burst from every direction, and I found myself instantly overwhelmed by some deadly weight, which prostrated me on the earth, and deprived me of sense and motion.

I know not how long I continued in this state; but I remember that, on opening my eyes, the first object that presented itself to me was the sky, glowing as before with ten thousand stars, and the moon walking in her unclouded brightness through the heavens. The whole circumstance then rushed back upon my mind, but with a sense of horror very much diminished. I arose, and on looking towards the spot, perceived the coffin in the same place. I then stood, and endeavouring to collect myself, viewed it as calmly as possible; it was, however, as motionless and distinct as when I first saw it. I now began to reason upon the matter, and to consider that it was pusillanimous in me to give way to such boyish terrors. The confidence, also, which my heart, only a short time before this, had experienced in the presence and protection of the Almighty, again returned, and, along with it, a degree of religious fortitude which invigorated my whole system. "Well," thought I, "in the name of God I shall ascertain what you are, let the consequence be what it may." I then advanced until I stood exactly over it, and raising my foot, gave it a slight kick. "Now," said I, "nothing remains but to ascertain whether it contains a dead body or not," but on raising the end of it I perceived by its lightness that it was empty. To investigate the cause of its being left in this solitary spot was, however, not within the compass of my philosophy, so I gave that up. On looking at it more closely I noticed a plate marked with the name and age of the person for whom it was intended, and on bringing my eye near the letters, I was able, between fingering and reading, to make out the name of my old cudgel-fighting schoolfellow, Denis Kelly.

This discovery threw a partial light upon the business; but I now remembered to have heard of individuals who had seen black, unearthly coffins inscribed with the names of certain living persons, and that these were considered as ominous of the death of those persons. I accordingly determined to be certain that this was a real coffin; and as Denis's house was not more than a mile before me, I decided on carrying it that far. "If he be dead," thought I, "it will be all right; and if not, we will see more about it." My mind, in fact, was diseased with terror. I instantly raised the coffin, and as I found a rope lying on the ground under it, I strapped it about my shoulders and proceeded; nor could I help smiling when I reflected upon the singular transition which the man of sentiment and sensation so strangely underwent—from the sublime contemplation of the silent mountain solitude and the spangled heavens to the task of carrying a coffin. It was an adventure, however, and I was resolved to see how it would terminate.

There was from the bridge an ascent in the road, not so gradual as that by which I descended on the other side; and as the coffin was rather heavy, I began to repent of having anything to do with it, for I was by no means experienced in carrying coffins. The carriage of it was, indeed, altogether an irksome and unpleasant concern; for owing to my ignorance of using the rope that tied it skilfully, it was every moment sliding down my back, dragging along the stones, or bumping against my heels; besides, I saw no sufficient grounds I had for entering upon the ludicrous and odd employment of

13

carrying another man's coffin, and was several times upon the point of washing my hands out of it altogether. But the novelty of the incident, and the mystery in which it was involved, decided me in bringing it as far as Kelly's house, which was exactly on my way home.

I had yet half a mile to go; but I thought it would be best to strap it more firmly about my body before I could start again. I therefore set it standing on its end, just at the turn of the road, until I should breathe a little, for I was rather exhausted by a trudge under it of half a mile and upwards. Whilst the coffin was in this position, I standing exactly behind it (Kelly had been a tall man, consequently it was somewhat higher than I was), a crowd of people bearing lights advanced round the corner, and the first object which presented itself to their vision was the coffin in that position, whilst I was totally invisible behind it. As soon as they saw it there was an involuntary cry of consternation from the whole crowd. At this time I had the coffin once more strapped firmly by a running knot to my shoulders, so that I could loose it whenever I pleased. On seeing the party, and hearing certain expressions which dropped from them, I knew at once that there had been some unlucky blunder in the business on their part; and I would have given a good deal to be out of the circumstances in which I then stood. I felt that I could not possibly have accounted for my situation without bringing myself in for as respectable a portion of rank cowardice as those who ran away from the coffin; for that it was left behind in a fit of terror I now entertained no doubt whatever, particularly when I remembered the traditions connected with the spot in which I found it.

"*Manim a Yea agus a wurrah!*" exclaimed one of them, "if the black man hasn't brought it up from the bridge— *dher a lorna heena*, he did; for it was above the bridge we first seen him : jist for all the world—the Lord be about us— as Antony and me war coming out on the road at the bridge, there he was standing—a headless man, all black, widout face or eyes upon him—and then we cut acrass the fields home."

"But where is he now, Eman?" said one of them. "Are you sure you seen him ?"

14

"Seen him!" both exclaimed; "do ye think we'd take to our scrapers like two hares, only we did? Arrah, bad manners to you, do you think the coffin could walk up wid itself from the bridge to this, only he brought it?—isn't that enough?"

"Thrue for yees," the rest exclaimed; "but what's to be done?"

"Why, to bring the coffin home, now that we're all together," another observed. "They say he never appears to more than two at wanst, so he won't be apt to show himself now."

"Well, boys, let two of you go down to it," said one of them, "and we'll wait here till yees bring it up."

"Yes," said Eman Dhu, "do you go down, Owen, as you have the scapular [1] on you, and the jug of holy water in your hand, and let Billy M'Shane, here, repate the confeethur [2] along wid you."

"Isn't it the same thing, Eman," replied Owen, "if I shake the holy water on you and whoever goes wid you : sure, you know that if only one dhrop of it touched you, the divil himself couldn't harm you!"

"And what needs yourself be afraid, then," retorted Eman, "and you has the scapular on you to the back of that? Didn't you say, as you war coming out, that if it was the divil you'd disparse him?"

"You had betther not be mintioning his name, you *omadhaun*," replied the other. "If I was your age, and hadn't a wife and childher on my hands, it's myself that would trust in God and go down manfully; but the people are henhearted now besides what they used to be in my time."

During this conversation I had resolved, if possible, to keep up the delusion until I could get myself extricated with due secrecy out of this ridiculous situation; and I was glad to find that, owing to their cowardice, there was some likelihood of effecting my design.

"Ned," said one of them to a little man, "go down and speak to it, as it can't harm *you*."

"Why, sure," said Ned, with a tremor in his voice, "I can

---

[1] A blessed object worn on the body to keep away evil.
[2] "Confiteor."

15

speak to it where I am, widout going within rache of it. Boys, stay close to me—hem—In the name of—But don't you think I had betther spake to it in the Latin I sarve mass wid? it can't but answer that, for the sowl of it, seeing it's a blest language."

"Very well," the rest replied; "try that, Ned; give it the best and ginteelest grammar you have, and maybe it may thrate us dacent."

Now it so happened that in my schoolboy days I had joined, from mere frolic, a class of young fellows who were learning what is called the "Sarvin' of Mass," and had impressed it so accurately on a pretty retentive memory that I never forgot it. At length Ned pulled out his beads, and bedewed himself most copiously with the holy water. He then shouted out, with a voice which resembled that of a man in an ague fit—"*Dóm-i-n-us vo-bis-cum?*" "*Et cum spiritu tuo,*" I replied, in a husky, sepulchral tone, from behind the coffin. As soon as I uttered these words the whole crowd ran back instinctively with affright; and Ned got so weak that they were obliged to support him.

"Lord have marcy on us!" said Ned. "Boys, isn't it an awful thing to speak to a spirit! My hair is like I dunno what, it's sticking up so stiff upon my head."

"Spake to it in English, Ned," said they, "till we hear what it will say. Ax it does anything trouble it, or whether its sowl's in purgatory."

"Wouldn't it be betther," observed another, "to ax it who murdhered it?—maybe it wants to discover that."

"In the—na-me of go-o-d-ness," said Ned, down to me, "what are you?"

"I'm the soul," I replied in the same voice, "of the pedlar that was murdered on the bridge below."

"And—who—was—it, sur, wid—submission, that—murdhered—you?"

To this I made no reply.

"I say," continued Ned, "in—the—name—of—g-o-o-d-ness—who was it—that took the liberty of murdhering you, dacent man?"

"Ned Corrigan," I answered, giving his own name.

"Hem! God presarve us! Ned Corrigan!" he exclaimed,

16

"What Ned, for there's two of them? Is it myself, or the other vagabone?"

"Yourself, you murderer!" I replied.

"Ho!" said Ned, getting quite stout—"is that you, neighbour? Come now, walk out wid yourself out of that coffin, you vagabone you, whoever you are."

"What do you mane, Ned, by spaking to it that a-away?" the rest inquired.

"Hut," said Ned, "it's some fellow or other that's playing a thrick upon us. Sure, I never knew neither act nor part of the murdher nor of the murdherers; and you know, if it was anything of that nature, it couldn't tell me a lie, and me a scapularian, along wid axing it in God's name, wid Father Feasthalagh's Latin."

"Big tare-an-ouns!" said the rest, "if we thought it was any man making fun of us, but we'd crop the ears off his head, to tache him to be joking!"

To tell the truth, when I heard this suggestion I began to repent of my frolic; but I was determined to make another effort to finish the adventure creditably.

"Ned," said they, "throw some of the holy water on us all, and in the name of St. Pether and the Blessed Virgin we'll go down and examine it in a body."

This they considered a good thought, and Ned was sprinkling the water about him in all directions, whilst he repeated some jargon which was completely unintelligible. They then began to approach the coffin at dead-march time, and I felt that this was the only moment in which my plan could succeed, for had I waited until they came down, all would have been discovered. As soon, therefore, as they began to move towards me, I also began, with equal solemnity, to retrograde towards them; so that as the coffin was between us, it seemed to move without human means.

"Stop, for God's sake—stop!" shouted Ned; "it's movin'! It has made the coffin alive; don't you see it stepping this way widout hand or foot, barring the boords!"

There was now a halt to ascertain the fact; but I still retrograded. This was sufficient—a cry of terror broke from the whole group, and without waiting for further evidence they set off in the direction they came from, at full speed,

17

Ned flinging the jug of holy water at the coffin, lest the latter should follow, or the former encumber him in his flight. Never was there so complete a discomfiture; and so eager were they to escape that several of them came down on the stones, and I could hear them shouting with desperation, and imploring the more advanced not to leave them behind. I instantly disentangled myself from the coffin, and left it standing exactly in the middle of the road, for the next passenger to give it a lift as far as Denis Kelly's, if he felt so disposed. I lost no time in making the best of my way home; and on passing poor Denis's house, I perceived, by the bustle and noise within, that he was dead.

I had given my friends no notice of this visit; my reception was consequently the warmer, as I was not expected. That evening was a happy one, which I shall long remember. At supper I alluded to Kelly, and received from my brother a full account, as given in the following narrative, of the circumstances which caused his death.

"I need not remind you, Toby, of our schoolboy days, nor of the principles usually imbibed at such schools as that in which the two tiny factions of the Caseys and the Murphys qualified themselves—among the latter of whom you cut so distinguished a figure. You will not, therefore, be surprised to hear that those two factions are as bitter as ever, and that the boys who at Pat Mulligan's school belaboured each other, in imitation of their brothers and fathers, continue to set the same iniquitous example to their children; so that this groundless and hereditary enmity is likely to descend to future generations—unless, indeed, the influence of a more enlightened system of education may check it. But, unhappily, there is a strong suspicion of the object proposed by such a system; so that the advantages likely to result from it to the lower orders of the people will be slow and distant."

"But, John," said I, "now that we are upon that subject, let me ask what really is the bone of contention between Irish factions?"

"I assure you," he replied, "I am almost as much at a loss, Toby, to give you a satisfactory answer as if you asked me the elevation of the highest mountain on the moon; and

I believe you would find equal difficulty in ascertaining the cause of the feuds from the factions themselves. I really am convinced they know not, nor, if I rightly understand them, do they much care. Their object is to fight, and the turning of a straw will at any time furnish them with sufficient grounds for that. I do not think, after all, that the enmity between them is purely personal: they do not hate each other individually; but having originally had one quarrel upon some trifling occasion, the beaten party could not bear the stigma of defeat without another trial of strength. Then if they succeed, the *onus* of retrieving lost credit is thrown upon the party that was formerly victorious. If they fail a second time, the double triumph of their conquerors excites them to a greater determination to throw off the additional disgrace; and this species of alternation perpetuates the evil.

"These habits, however, familiarise our peasantry to acts of outrage and violence—the bad passions are cultivated and nourished, until crimes, which peaceable men look upon with fear and horror, lose their real magnitude and deformity in the eyes of Irishmen. I believe this kind of undefined hatred between either parties or nations is the most dangerous and fatal spirit which could pervade any portion of society. If you hate a man for an obvious and palpable injury, it is likely that when he cancels that injury by an act of subsequent kindness, accompanied by an exhibition of sincere sorrow, you will cease to look upon him as your enemy; but where the hatred is such that, while feeling it, you cannot, on a sober examination of your heart, account for it, there is little hope that you will ever be able to stifle the enmity which you entertain against him. This, however, in politics and religion is what is frequently designated as principle—a word on which men possessing higher and greater advantages than the poor ignorant peasantry of Ireland pride themselves. In sects and parties we may mark its effects among all ranks and nations. I therefore seldom wish, Toby, to hear a man assert that he is of this party or that from principle; for I am usually inclined to suspect that he is not in this case influenced by conviction.

"Kelly was a man who, but for these scandalous proceedings among us, might have been now alive and happy.

Although his temperament was warm, yet that warmth communicated itself to his good as well as to his evil qualities. In the beginning his family were not attached to any faction —and when I use the word faction it is in contradistinction to the word party'; for faction, you know, is applied to a feud or grudge between Roman Catholics exclusively. But when he was young he ardently attached himself to the Murphys; and having continued among them until manhood, he could not abandon them consistently with that sense of mistaken honour which forms so prominent a feature in the character of Irish peasantry. But although the Kellys were not faction men, they were bitter party men, being the ringleaders of every quarrel which took place between the Catholics and Protestants, or, I should rather say, between the Orangemen and Whiteboys.

" From the moment when Denis attached himself to the Murphys until the day he received the beating which subsequently occasioned his death, he never withdrew from them. He was in all their battles; and in course of time induced his relations to follow his example; so that, by general consent, they were nicknamed 'the Errigle Slashers.' Soon after you left the country, and went to reside with my uncle, Denis married a daughter of little Dick Magrath's, from the Race-road, with whom he got a little money. She proved a kind, affectionate wife; and, to do him justice, I believe he was an excellent husband. Shortly after his marriage his father died, and Denis succeeded him in his farm; for you know that among the peasantry the youngest usually gets the landed property—the elder children being obliged to provide for themselves according to their ability, or otherwise a population would multiply upon a portion of land inadequate to their support.

" It was supposed that Kelly's marriage would have been the means of producing a change in him for the better, but it did not. He was, in fact, the slave of a low, vain ambition which constantly occasioned him to have some quarrel or other on his hands; and as he possessed great physical courage and strength, he became the champion of the parish. It was in vain that his wife used every argument to induce him to relinquish such practices; the only reply he was in the habit of making was a good-humoured slap on the back and a laugh, saying—

"'That's it, Honor; sure and isn't that the Magraths all over, that would let the manest *spalpeen* that ever chewed cheese thramp upon them widout raising a hand in their own defence; and I don't blame you for being a coward, seeing that you have their blood in your veins—not but that there ought to be something betther in you, afther all; for it's the M'Carrons, by your mother's side, that had the good dhrop of their own in them, anyhow—but you're a Magrath, out and out.'

"'And, Denis,' Honor would reply, 'it would be a blessed day for the parish if all in it were as peaceable as the same Magraths. There would be no sore heads, nor broken bones, nor fighting, nor slashing of one another in fairs and markets, when people ought to be minding their business. You're ever and always at the Magraths, bekase they don't join you agin the Caseys or the Orangemen, and more fools they'd be to make or meddle between you, having no spite agin either of them; and it would be wiser for you to be sed by the Magraths, and red your hands out of sich ways altogether. What did ever the Murphys do to sarve you or any of your family, that you'd go to make a great man of yourself fighting for them? Or what did the poor Caseys do to make you go agin the honest people? Arrah, bad manners to me, if you know what you're about, or if sonse[1] or grace can ever come of it; and mind my words, Denis, if God hasn't sed it, you'll live to rue your folly for the same work.'

" At this Denis would laugh heartily. 'Well said Honor Magrath, but not Kelly. Well, it's one comfort that our childher aren't likely to follow your side of the house, anyway. Come here, Lanty—come over, *acushla,* to your father! Lanty, *ma bouchal,* what 'ill you do when you grow a man?'

"'I'll buy a horse of my own to ride on, daddy.'

"'A horse, Lanty!—and so you will, *ma bouchal;* but that's not it—sure, that's not what I mane, Lanty. What 'ill you do to the Caseys?'

"'Ho, ho! the Caseys!—I'll bate the blackguards wid your blackthorn, daddy!'

[1] Good luck.

21

"'Ha, ha, ha!—that's my stout man—my brave little sodger! *Wus dha lamh avick!*—give me your hand, my son! Here, Nelly,' he would say to the child's eldest sister, 'give him a brave whang of bread, to make him able to bate the Caseys. Well, Lanty, who more will you leather, *ahagur?*'

"'All the Orangemen—I'll kill all the Orangemen!'

"This would produce another laugh from the father, who would again kiss and shake hands with his son for these early manifestations of his own spirit.

"'Lanty, *ma bouchal*,' he would say, 'thank God you're not a Magrath; 'tis you that's a Kelly, every blessed inch of you! —and if you turn out as good a *builla batthah* as your father afore you, I'll be contint, *avourneen!*'

"'God forgive you, Denis,' the wife would reply—'it's long before you'd think of larning him his prayers, or his catechism, or anything that's good! Lanty, *agra*, come over to myself, and never heed what that man says; for, except you have some poor body's blessing, he'll bring you to no good.'

"Sometimes, however, Kelly's own natural good sense, joined with the remonstrances of his wife, prevailed for a short time, and he would withdraw himself from the connection altogether; but the force of habit and of circumstances was too strong in him to hope that he could ever overcome it by his own firmness, for he was totally destitute of religion. The peaceable intervals of his life were therefore very short.

"One summer evening I was standing in my own garden, when I saw a man galloping up towards me at full speed. When he approached I recognised him as one of the Murphy faction, and perceived that he was cut and bleeding.

"'Murphy,' said I, 'what's the matter?'

"'Hard fighting, sir,' said he, 'is the matter. The Caseys gathered all their faction, bekase they heard that Denis Kelly has given us up, and they're sweeping the street wid us. I'm going hot foot for Kelly, sir, for even the very name of him will turn the tide in our favour. Along wid that, I have sint in a score of the Duggans, and if I get in Denis, plase God, we'll clear the town of them!'

"He then set off, but pulled up abruptly, and said—

"'*Arrah*, Mr. Darcy, maybe you'd be civil enough to lind

me the loan of a sword, or bagnet, or gun, or anything that way, that would be sarviceable to a body on a pinch ? '

" ' Yes ! ' said I, ' and enable you to commit murder. No, no, Murphy ! I'm sorry it's not in my power to put a final stop to such dangerous quarrels.'

" He then dashed off, and in the course of a short time I saw him and Kelly, both on horseback, hurrying into the town in all possible haste, armed with their cudgels. The following day I got my dog and gun, and sauntered about the hills, making a point to call upon Kelly. I found him with his head tied up, and his arm in a sling.

" ' Well, Denis,' said I, ' I find you have kept your promise of giving up quarrels ! '

" ' And so I did, sir,' said Denis ; ' but, sure, you wouldn't have me go for to desart them, when the Caseys war three to one over them. No ; God be thanked, I'm not so mane as that, anyhow. Besides, they welted both my brothers within an inch of their lives.'

" I think they didn't miss yourself,' said I.

" ' You may well say they did not, sir,' he replied ; ' and, to tell God's thruth, they thrashed us right and left out of the town, although we rallied three times and came in again. At any rate, it's the first time for the last five years that they dare go up and down the street calling out for the face of a Murphy or a Kelly—for they're as bitter now agin us as agin the Murphys themselves.'

" ' Well, I hope, Denis,' I observed, ' that what occurred yesterday will prevent you from entering into their quarrels in future. Indeed, I shall not give over until I prevail on you to lead a quiet and peaceable life, as the father of a rising family ought to do.'

" ' Denis,' said the wife, when I alluded to the children, looking at him with a reproachful and significant expression— ' Denis, do you hear that ?—the father of a family, Denis ! Oh, then, God look down on that family, but it's—*Musha*, God bless you and yours, sir,' said she to me, dropping that part of the subject abruptly. ' It's kind of you to trouble yourself about him, at all, at all ; it's what them that has a betther right to do it doesn't do.'

" ' I hope,' said I, ' that Denis's own good sense will show

23

him the folly and guilt of his conduct, and that he will not, under any circumstances, enter into their battles in future. Come, Denis, will you promise me this?'

"'If any man,' replied Denis, 'could make me do it, it's yourself, sir, or any one of your family; but if the priest of the parish was to go down on his two knees before me, I wouldn't give it up till we give them vagabone Caseys one glorious battherin', which, plase God, we'll do, and are well able to do, before a month of Sundays goes over us. Now, sir, you needn't say another word,' said he, seeing me about to speak, 'for, by Him that made me, we'll do it. If any man, I say, could persuade me agin it, you could; but if we don't pay them full interest for what we got, why, my name's not Denis Kelly—ay, sweep them like varmint out of the town, body and sleeves!'

"I saw argument would be lost on him, so I only observed that I feared it would eventually end badly.

"'Och, many and many's the time, Mr. Darcy,' said Honor, 'I prophesied the same thing; and if God hasn't said it, he'll be coming home a corpse to me some day or other, for he got as much bating, sir, as would be enough to kill a horse; and to tell you God's truth, sir, he's breeding up his childher——'

"'Honor,' said Kelly, irritated, 'whatever I do, do I lave it in your power to say that I'm a bad husband? so don't rise me by your talk, for I don't like to be provoked. I know it's wrong, but what can I do? Would you have me for to show the *garran bane*,[1] and lave them like a cowardly thraitor, now that the other faction is coming up to be their match? No; let what will come of it, I'll never do the mane thing—death before dishonour!'

"In this manner Kelly went on for years—sometimes, indeed, keeping quiet for a short period, but eventually drawn in, from the apprehension of being reproached with want of honour and truth to his connection. This, truly, is an imputation which no peasant could endure; nor, were he thought capable of treachery, would his life be worth a single

[1] The white horse, *i.e.*, be wanting in mettle. Carleton says the origin of the phrase is attributable to the tradition that James II. fled from the field at the Boyne on a white horse.

week's purchase. Many a time have I seen Kelly reeling home, his head and face sadly cut, the blood streaming from him, and his wife and some neighbour on each side of him — the poor woman weeping, and deploring the senseless and sanguinary feuds in which her husband took so active a part.

"About three miles from this, down at the Long Ridge, where the Shannons live, dwelt a family of the M'Guigans, cousins to Denis. They were anything but industrious, although they might have lived very independently, having held a farm on what they call an old take, which means a long lease taken out when the lands were cheap. It so happened, however, that, like too many of their countrymen, they paid little attention to the cultivation of their farm, the consequence of which neglect was that they became embarrassed and overburdened with arrears. Their landlord was old Sam Simmons, whose only fault to his tenants was an excess of indulgence, and a generous disposition, wherever he could possibly get an opportunity, to scatter his money about him, upon the spur of a benevolence which it would seem never ceased goading him to acts of the most Christian liberality and kindness. Along with these excellent qualities, he was remarkable for a most rooted aversion to law and lawyers; for he would lose one hundred pounds rather than recover that sum by legal proceedings, even when certain that five pounds would effect it; but he seldom or never was known to pardon a breach of the peace.

"I have always found that an excess of indulgence in a landlord never fails ultimately to injure and relax the industry of the tenant; at least, this was the effect which his forbearance produced on them. But the most extraordinary good-nature has its limits, and so had his; after repeated warning, and the most unparalleled patience on his part, he was at length compelled to determine on at once removing them from his estate, and letting his land to some more efficient and deserving tenant. He accordingly desired them to remove their property from the premises, as he did not wish, he said, to leave them without the means of entering upon another farm, if they felt so disposed. This they refused to do, adding that they would at least put him to the

25

expense of ejecting them. He then gave orders to his agent to seize; but they, in the meantime, had secreted their effects by night among their friends and relations, sending a cow to this one, and a horse to that; so that when the bailiff came to levy his execution he found very little except the empty walls. They were, however, ejected without ceremony, and driven altogether off the farm, for which they had actually paid nothing for the three preceding years. In the meantime the farm was advertised to be let, and several persons had offered themselves as tenants; but what appeared very remarkable was that the Roman Catholics seldom came a second time to make any further inquiry about it; or if they did, Simmons observed that they were sure to withdraw their proposals, and ultimately decline having anything to do with it.

"This was a circumstance which he could not properly understand; but the fact was that the peasantry were, to a man, members of a widely-extending system of Whiteboyism, the secret influence of which intimidated such of their own religion as intended to take it, and prevented them from exposing themselves to the penalty which they knew those who should dare to occupy it must pay. In a short time, however, the matter began to be whispered about, until it spread gradually, day after day, through the parish, that those who already had proposed, or intended to propose, were afraid to enter upon the land on any terms. Hitherto, it is true, these threats floated about only in the invisible form of rumour.

"The farm had been now unoccupied for about a year. Party spirit ran very high among the peasantry, and no proposals came in, or were at all likely to come. Simmons then got advertisements printed, and had them posted up in the most conspicuous parts of this and the neighbouring parishes. It was expected, however, that they would be torn down; but, instead of that, there was a written notice posted up immediately under each, which ran in the following words:—

"'TAKE NOTESS.

" ' Any man that'll dare to take the farm belonging to yallow Sam Simmons, and sitivated at the long ridge, will be flayed alive.

"'MAT MIDNIGHT.

" ' N.B.—It's it that was latterally occupied by the M'Guigans.'

" This occasioned Simmons and the other magistrates of the barony to hold a meeting, at which they subscribed to the amount of fifty pounds as a reward for discovering the author or authors of the threatening notice; but the advertisement containing the reward, which was posted in the usual places through the parish, was torn down on the first night after it was put up. In the meantime a man nicknamed Vengeance—Vesey Vengeance, in consequence of his daring and fearless spirit, and his bitterness in retaliating injury—came to Simmons, and proposed for the farm. The latter candidly mentioned the circumstances of the notice, and fairly told him that he was running a personal risk in taking it.

"'Leave that to me, sir,' said Vengeance; 'if you will set me the farm at the terms I offer, I am willing to become your tenant; and let them that posted up the notices go to old Nick, or if they annoy me, let them take care I don't send them there. I am a true-blue, sir—a purple man [1]— have lots of firearms, and plenty of stout fellows in the parish ready and willing to back me; and, by the light of day ! if they make or meddle with me or mine, we will hunt them in the face of the world, like so many mad dogs, out of the country. What are they but a pack of ribils, that would cut our throats if they dared ! '

"'I have no objection,' said Simmons, 'that you should express a firm determination to defend your life and protect your property; but I utterly condemn the spirit with which you seem to be animated. Be temperate and sober, but be firm. I will afford you every assistance and protection in my

[1] These terms denote certain stages of initiation in the Orange system.

27

power, both as a magistrate and a landlord ; but if you speak
so incautiously, the result may be serious, if not fatal, to
yourself.'

" ' Instead of that,' said Vengeance, ' the more a man
appears to be afeard, the more danger he is in, as I know
by what I have seen ; but, at any rate, if they injure me, I
wouldn't ask better sport than taking down the ribils—the
bloody-minded villains ! Isn't it a purty thing that a man
darn't put one foot past the other, only as they wish ? By
the light of day, I'll pepper them ! '

Shortly after this, Vengeance, braving all their threats,
removed to the farm, and set about its cultivation with skill
and vigour. He had not been long there, however, when a
notice was posted one night on his door, giving him ten days
to clear off from this interdicted spot, threatening, in case of
non-compliance, to make a bonfire of the house and offices,
inmates included. The reply which Vengeance made to this
was fearless and characteristic. He wrote another notice,
which he posted on the chapel door, stating that he would
not budge an inch—recommending, at the same time, such
as intended paying him a nightly visit to be careful that they
might not chance to go home with their heels foremost. This
indeed was setting them completely at defiance, and would
no doubt have been fatal to Vesey, were it not for a circumstance which I will now relate. In a little dell below Vesey's
house lived a poor woman called Doran, a widow ; she in-
habited a small hut, and was principally supported by her
two sons, who were servants—one to a neighbouring farmer,
a Roman Catholic, and the other to Dr. Ableson, rector of
the parish. He who had been with the rector lost his health
shortly before Vengeance succeeded the M'Guigans as occu-
pier of the land in question, and was obliged to come home
to his mother. He was then confined to his bed, from which,
indeed, he never rose.

" This boy had been his mother's principal support—for
the other was unsettled, and paid her but little attention,
being, like most of those in his situation, fond of drinking,
dancing, and attending fairs. In short, he became a Ribbon-
man, and consequently was obliged to attend their nightly
meetings. Now it so happened that for a considerable time

after the threatening notice had been posted on Vengeance's door, he received no annoyance, although the period allowed for his departure had been long past, and the purport of the paper uncomplied with. Whether this proceeded from an apprehension on the part of the Ribbonmen of receiving a warmer welcome than they might wish, or whether they deferred the execution of their threat until Vengeance might be off his guard, I cannot determine; but the fact is that some months had elapsed and Vengeance remained hitherto unmolested.

"During this interval the distress of Widow Doran had become known to the inmates of his family, and his mother —for she lived with him—used to bring down each day some nourishing food to the sick boy. In these kind offices she was very punctual; and so great was the poverty of the poor widow, and so destitute the situation of her sick son, that, in fact, the burden of their support lay principally upon Vengeance's family.

"Vengeance was a small, thin man, with fair hair and fiery eyes; his voice was loud and shrill, his utterance rapid, and the general expression of his countenance irritable; his motions were so quick that he rather seemed to run than walk. He was a civil, obliging neighbour, but performed his best actions with a bad grace; a firm, unflinching friend, but a bitter and implacable enemy. Upon the whole, he was generally esteemed and respected—though considered as an eccentric character, for such, indeed, he was. On hearing of Widow Doran's distress, he gave orders that a portion of each meal should be regularly sent down to her and her son; and from that period forward they were both supported principally from his table.

"In this way some months had passed, and still Vengeance was undisturbed in his farm. It often happened, however, that Doran's other son came to see his brother; and during these visits it was but natural that his mother and brother should allude to the kindness which they daily experienced from Vesey.

"One night, about twelve o'clock, a tap came to Widow Doran's door, who happened to be attending the invalid, as he was then nearly in the last stage of his illness. When she opened it, the other son entered, in an evident hurry, having the appearance of a man who felt deep and serious anxiety.

"'Mother,' said he, 'I was very uneasy entirely about Mick, and just started over to see him, although they don't know at home that I'm out, so I can't stay a crack; but I wish you would go to the door for two or three minutes, as I have something to say to him.'

"'Why, thin, Holy Mother!—Jack, *ahagur*, is there anything the matther, for you look as if you had seen something?'[1]

"'Nothing worse than myself, mother,' he replied; 'nor there's nothing the matther at all—only I have a few words to say to Mick here, that's all.'

"The mother accordingly removed herself out of hearing.

"'Mick,' says the boy, 'this is a bad business—I wish to God I was clear and clane out of it.'

"'What is it?' said Mick, alarmed.

"'Murther, I'm afeard, if God doesn't turn it off them somehow.'

"'What do you mane, man, at all?' said the invalid, raising himself, in deep emotion, on his elbow, from his poor straw bed.

"'Vengeance,' said he—'Vengeance, man—he's going to get it. I was out with the boys on Sunday evening, and at last it's agreed on to visit him to-morrow night. I'm sure and sartin he'll never escape, for there's more in for him than taking the farm, and daring them so often as he did—he shot two fingers off of a brother-in-law of Jem Reilly's one night that they war on for threshing him, and that's coming home to him along with the rest.'

"'In the name of God, Jack,' inquired Mick, 'what do you intend to do with him?'

"'Why,' replied Jack, 'it's agreed to put a coal in the thatch, in the first place; and although they were afeard to name what he's to get besides, I doubt they'll make a spatch-cock of himself. They won't meddle with any other of the family, though—but he's down for it.'

"'Are you to be one of them?' asked Mick.

---

[1] *Something—i.e.,* a ghost or such-like.

"'I was the third man named,' replied the other, 'bekase, they said, I knew the place.'

"'Jack,' said his emaciated brother, with much solemnity, raising himself up in the bed—'Jack, if you have act or part in that bloody business, God in His glory you'll never see. Fly the country—cut off a finger or toe—break your arm— or do something that may prevent you from being there. Oh, my God!' he exclaimed, whilst the tears fell fast down his pale cheeks—'to go to murdher the man, and lave his little family widout a head or a father over them, and his wife a widow! To burn his place, widout rhyme, or rason, or offince. Jack, if you go, I'll die cursing you. I'll appear to you—I'll let you rest neither night nor day, sleeping nor waking, in bed or out of bed. I'll haunt you till you'll curse the very day you war born.'

"'Whisht, Micky,' said Jack, 'you're frightening me. I'll not go—will that satisfy you?'

"'Well, dhrop down on your two knees there,' said Micky, 'and swear, before the God that has His eye upon you, this minute, that you'll have no hand in injuring him or his while you live. If you don't do this, I'll not rest in my grave, and maybe I'll be a corpse before mornin'.'

"'Well, Micky,' said Jack, who, though wild and un-thinking, was a lad whose heart and affections were good, 'it would be hard for me to refuse you that much, and you not likely to be long with me—I will,' and he accordingly knelt down and swore solemnly, in words which his brother dictated to him, that he would not be concerned in the intended murder.

"'Now give me your hand, Jack,' said the invalid; 'God bless you—and so He will. Jack, if I depart before I see you again, I'll die happy. That man has supported me and my mother for near the last three months, bad as you all think him. Why, Jack, we would both be dead of hunger long ago, only for his family—and, my God! to think of such a murdhering intention makes my blood run cowld.'

"'You had better give him a hint, then,' said Jack, 'some way, or he'll be done for, as sure as you're stretched on that bed; but don't mintion names, if you wish to keep me from being murdhered for what I did. I must be off now, for I

31

stole out of the barn; [1] and only that Atty Laghy's gone along wid the master to the ⸺ fair, to help him sell the two coults, I couldn't get over at all.'

"'Well, go home, Jack, and God bless you, and so He will, for what you did this night.'

"Jack accordingly departed after bidding his mother and brother farewell.

"When the old woman came in, she asked her son if there was anything wrong with his brother; but he replied that there was not.

"'Nothing at all,' said he; 'but will you go up airly in the morning, plase God, and tell Vesey Johnston that I want to see him; and—that—I have a great dale to say to him.'

"'To be sure I will, Micky; but, Lord guard us, what ails you, *avourneen*, you look so frightened?'

"'Nothing at all, at all, mother; but will you go where I say airly to-morrow, for me?'

"'It's the first thing I'll do, God willin',' replied the mother. And the next morning Vesey was down with the invalid very early, for the old woman kept her word, and paid him a timely visit.

"'Well, Micky, my boy,' said Vengeance, as he entered the hut, 'I hope you're no worse this morning.'

"'Not worse, sir,' replied Mick; 'nor, indeed, am I anything better either, but much the same way. Sure, it's I that knows very well that my time here is but short.'

"'Well, Mick, my boy,' said Vengeance, 'I hope you're prepared for death, and that you expect forgiveness, like a Christian. Look up, my boy, to God at once, and pitch the priests and their craft to ould Nick, where they'll all go at the long-run.'

"'I blieve,' said Mick, with a faint smile, 'that you're not very fond of the priests, Mr. Johnston; but if you knew the power they possess as well as I do, you wouldn't spake of them so bad, anyhow.'

"'Me fond of them!' replied the other; 'why, man, they're a set of the most gluttonous, black-looking hypocrites that ever walked on neat's leather, and ought to be hunted out of

---

[1] Labouring servants in Ireland usually sleep in barns.

the country—hunted out of the country, by the light of day, every one of them; for they do nothing but egg up the people against the Protestants.'

" 'God help you, Mr. Johnston,' replied the invalid; 'I pity you from my heart for the opinion you hould about the blessed crathurs. I suppose if you were sthruck dead on the spot wid a blast from the fairies, that you think a priest couldn't cure you by one word's spaking?'

" 'Cure me!' said Vengeance, with a laugh of disdain; 'by the light of day, if I caught one of them curing me, I'd give him the purtiest chase you ever saw in your life across the hills.'

" 'Don't you know,' said Mick, 'that priest Dannelly cured Bob Arthurs of the falling sickness, until he broke the vow that was laid upon him of not going into a church; and the minute he crossed the church-door didn't he dhrop down as bad as ever—and what could the minister do for him?'

" 'And don't *you* know,' rejoined Vengeance, 'that that's all a parcel of the most lying stuff possible—lies—lies—all lies —and vagabondism. Why, Mick, you Papishes worship the priests; you think they can bring you to heaven at a word. By the light of day, they must have good sport laughing at you when they get among one another. Why don't they teach you, and give you the Bible to read, the ribelly rascals?—but they're afraid you'd know too much then.'

" 'Well, Mr. Johnston,' said Mick, 'I blieve you'll never have a good opinion of them, at any rate.'

" 'Ay, when the sky falls,' replied Vengeance; 'but you're now on your deathbed, and why don't you pitch them to ould Nick, and get a Bible? Get a Bible, man. There's a pair of them in my house that's never used at all—except my mother's, and she's at it night and day. I'll send one of them down to you. Turn yourself to God—to your Redeemer, that died on the mount of Jehoshaphat, or somewhere about Jerusalem, for your sins—and don't go out of the world from the hand of a rascally priest, with a band about your eyes, as if you were at blind-man's-buff; for, by the light of day, you're as blind as a bat in a religious way."

" 'There's no use in sending me a Bible,' replied the invalid, 'for I can't read it; but, whatever you may think, I'm very willing to lave my salvation with my priest.'

"'Why, man,' observed Vengeance, 'I thought you were going to have sense at last, and that you sent for me to give you some spiritual consolation.'

"'No, sir,' replied Mick; 'I have two or three words to spake to you.'

"'Come, come, Mick; now that we're on a spiritual subject, I'll hear nothing from you till I try whether it's possible to give you a true insight into religion. Stop, now, and let us lay our heads together, that we may make out something of a dacenter creed for you to believe in than the one you profess. Tell me truth, do you believe in the priests?'

"'How?' replied Mick. 'I believe that they're holy men; but I know they can't save me widout the Redeemer and His blessed mother.'

"'By the light above us, you're shuffling, Mick; I say you do believe in them—now don't tell me to the contrary—I say you're shuffling as fast as possible.'

"'I tould you truth, sir,' replied Mick; 'and if you don't blieve me, I can't help it.'

"'Don't trust in the priests, Mick; that's the main point to secure your salvation.'

"Mick, who knew his prejudices against the priests, smiled faintly, and replied—

"'Why, sir, I trust in them as being able to make inthercession wid God for me, that's all.'

"'They make intercession! By the stool I'm sitting on, a single word from one of them would ruin you. They, a set of ribles, to make interest for you in heaven! Didn't they rise the rebellion in Ireland?—answer me that.'

"'This is a subject, sir, we would never agree on,' replied Mick.

"'Have you the Ten Commandments?' inquired Vesey.

"'I doubt my mimory's not clear enough to have them in my mind,' said the lad, feeling keenly the imputation of ignorance which he apprehended from Vesey's blunt observations.

"Vesey, however, had penetration enough to perceive his feelings, and, with more delicacy than could be expected from him, immediately moved the question.

"'No matter, Mick,' said he; 'if you would give up the

34

priests, we would get over that point. As it is, I'll give you a lift in the Commandments; and, as I said a while ago, if you take my advice, I'll work up a creed for you that you may depend upon. But now for the Commandments. Let me see.

"'First: Thou shalt have no other gods but Me. Don't you see, man, how that peppers the priests?

"'Second: Remember that thou keep holy the Sabbath day.

"'Third: Thou shalt not make to thyself—no—hang it, no—I'm out; that's the Second—very right. Third: Honour thy father and thy mother—you understand that, Mick? It means that you are bound to—to—just so—to honour your father and your mother, poor woman.'

"'My father—God be good to him—is dead near fourteen years, sir,' replied Mick.

"'Well, in that case, Mick, you see all that's left for you is to honour your mother—although I'm not certain of that either; the Commandments make no allowance at all for death, and in that case, why, living or dead, the surest way is to respect and obey them—that is—if the thing weren't impossible. I wish we had blind George M'Gin here, Mick; although he's as great a rogue as ever escaped hemp, yet he'd beat the devil himself at a knotty point.'

"'His breath would be bad about a dying man,' observed Mick.

"'Ay, or a living one,' said Vesey. 'However, let us get on —we were at the Third. Fourth: Thou shalt do no murder.'

"At the word murder, Mick started, and gave a deep groan, whilst his eyes and features assumed a great and hollow expression, resembling that of a man struck with an immediate sense of horror and affright.

"'Oh, for heaven's sake, sir, stop there!' said Doran; 'that brings to my mind the business I had with you, Mr. Johnston.'

"'What is it about?' inquired Vengeance, in his usual eager manner.

"'Do you mind,' said Mick, 'that a paper was stuck one night upon your door, threatening you if you wouldn't lave that farm you're in?'

35

"'I do—the bloodthirsty villains! but they knew a trick worth two of coming near me.'

"'Well,' said Mick, 'a strange man, that I had never seen before, come into me last night, and tould me, if I'd see you, to say that you would get a visit from the boys this night, and to take care of yourself.'

"'Give me the hand, Mick,' said Vengeance—'give me the hand. In spite of the priests, by the light of day, you're an honest fellow. This night, you say, they're to come? And what are the bloody wretches to do, Mick? But I needn't ask that, for I suppose it's to murder myself, and to burn my place.'

"'I'm afeard, sir, you're not far from the truth,' replied Mick. 'But, Mr. Johnston, for God's sake, don't mintion my name; for if you do, I'll get myself what they war laying out for you—be burned in my bed, maybe.'

"'Never fear, Mick,' replied Vengeance; 'your name will never cross my lips.'

"'It's a great thing,' said Mick, 'that would make me turn informer; but, sure, only for your kindness and the goodness of your family, the Lord spare you to one another, mightn't I be dead long ago? I couldn't have one minute's peace if you or yours came to any harm when I could prevint it.'

"'Say no more, Mick,' said Vengeance, taking his hand again. 'I know that; leave the rest to me. But how do you find yourself, my poor fellow? you look weaker than you did a good deal.'

"'Indeed, I'm going very fast, sir,' replied Mick; 'I know it'll soon be over with me.'

"'Hut, no, man,' said Vengeance, drawing his hand rapidly across his eyes, and clearing his voice. 'Not at all; don't say so. Would a little broth serve you? or a bit of fresh meat?—or would you have a fancy for anything that I could make out for you? I'll get you wine, if you think it would do you good.'

"'God reward you,' said Mick feebly—'God reward you, and open your eyes to the truth. Is my mother likely to come in, do you think?'

"'She must be here in a few minutes,' the other replied;

'she was waiting till they'd churn, that she might bring you down a little fresh milk and butter.'

"'I wish she was wid me,' said the poor lad, 'for I'm lonely wantin' her—her voice and the very touch of her hands goes to my heart. Mother, come to me—and let me lay my head upon your breast, *agra machree*, for I think it will be for the last time. We lived lonely, *avourneen*, wid none but ourselves—sometimes in happiness, when the nabours ud be kind to us; and sometimes in sorrow, when there ud be none to help us. It's all over now, mother, and I'm laving you for ever.'

"Vengeance wiped his eyes. 'Rouse yourself, Mick,' said he—'rouse yourself.'

"'Who is that sitting along with you on the stool?' said Mick.

"'No one,' replied his neighbour—'but what's the matter with you, Mick?—your face is changed.'

"Mick, however, made no reply; but after a few slight struggles, in which he attempted to call upon his mother's name, he breathed his last. When Vengeance saw that he was dead—looked upon the cold, miserable hut in which this grateful and affectionate young man was stretched—and then reflected on the important service he had just rendered him, he could not suppress his tears.

"After sending down some of the females to assist his poor mother in laying him out, Vengeance went among his friends and acquaintances, informing them of the intelligence he had received, without mentioning the source from which he had it. After dusk that evening they all flocked as privately as possible to his house, to the number of thirty or forty, well provided with arms and ammunition. Some of them stationed themselves in the outhouses, some behind the garden hedge, and others in the dwelling-house."

When my brother had got thus far in his narrative, a tap came to the parlour-door, and immediately a stout-looking man, having the appearance of a labourer, entered the room.

"Well, Lachlin," said my brother, "what's the matter?"

"Why, sir," said Lachlin, scratching his head, "I had a bit of a favour to ax, if it would be plasin' to you to grant it to me."

37

"What is that?" said my brother.

"Do you know, sir," said he, "I haven't been at a wake—let us see—this two or three years, anyhow, and if you'd have no objection, why, I'd slip up a while to Denis Kelly's; he's a distant relation of my own, sir; and blood's thicker than wather, you know."

"I'm just glad you came in, Lachlin," said my brother. "I didn't think of you—take a chair here, and never heed the wake to-night, but sit down and tell us about the attack on Vesey Vengeance long ago. I'll get you a tumbler of punch; and instead of going to the wake, I will allow you to go to the funeral to-morrow."

"Ah, sir," said Lachlin, "you know whenever the punch is consarned I'm aisily persuaded; but not making little of your tumbler, sir," said the shrewd fellow, "I would get two or three of them if I went to the wake."

"Well, sit down," said my brother, handing him one, "and we won't permit you to get thirsty while you're talking, at all events."

"In throth, you haven't your heart in the likes of it," said Lachlin. "Gintlemen, your healths—your health, sir, and we're happy to see you wanst more. Why, thin, I remember you, sir, when you were a *gorsoon*, passing to school wid your satchel on your back; but, I'll be bound, you're by no means as soople now as you were thin. Why, sir," turning to my brother, "he could fly, or kick football wid the rabbits. Well, this is raal stuff!"

"Now, Lachlin," said my brother, "give us an account of the attack you made on Vesey Vengeance's house at the Long Ridge, when all your party were chased out of the town."

"Why, thin, sir, I ought to be ashamed to mintion it; but you see, gintlemen, there was no getting over being connected wid them, for a man's life wouldn't be his own if he refused—but I hope your brother's safe, sir!"

"Oh, perfectly safe, Lachlin; you may rest assured he'll never mention it."

"Well, sir," said Lachlin, addressing himself to me, "Vesey Vengeance was——"

"Lachlin," said my brother, "he knows all about Vesey; just give an account of the attack."

38

"The attack, sir!—no, but the chivey we got over the mountains. Why, sir, we met in an ould empty house, you see, that belonged to the Farrells of Ballyboulteen, that went over to America that spring. There war none wid us, you may be sure, but them that war up; and in all we might be about sixty or seventy. The M'Guigans, one way or another, got it up first among them, bekase they expected that Mr. Simmons would take them back when he'd find that no one else dare venthur upon their land. There war at that time two fellows down from the county Longford, in their neighbourhood, of the name of Collier—although that wasn't their right name—they were here upon their keeping, for the murder of a proctor in their own part of the country. One of them was a tall, powerful fellow, with sandy hair and red brows; the other was a slender chap, that must have been drawn into it by his brother—for he was very mild and innocent, and always persuaded us agin evil. The M'Guigans brought lashings of whisky, and made them that war to go foremost amost drunk—these war the two Colliers, some of the strangers from behind the mountains, and a son of Widdy Doran's, that knew every inch about the place, for he was bred and born jist below the house a bit. He wasn't wid us, however, in regard of his brother being under boord that night; but instid of him Tim M'Guigan went to show the way up the little glin to the house—though, for that matther, the most of us knew as well as he did, but we didn't like to be the first to put a hand to it if we could help it.

"At any rate, we sot in Farrell's empty house, drinking whisky, till they war all gathered, when about two dozen of them got the damp soot from the chimley, and rubbed it over their faces, making them so black that their own relations couldn't know them. We then went across the country in little lots of about six, or ten, or a score; and we war glad that the wake was in Widdy Doran's, seeing that if any one would meet us, we war going to it, you know, and the blackening of the faces would pass for a frolic; but there was no great danger of being met, for it was now long beyant midnight.

"Well, gintlemen, it puts me into a tremble, even at this time, to think of how little we cared about doing what we

39

were bent upon. Them that had to manage the business war more than half drunk; and hard fortune to me, but you would think it was to a wedding they went—some of them singing songs aginst the law—some of them quite merry, and laughing as if they had found a mare's nest. The big fellow, Collier, had a dark lanthern wid a half-burned turf in it, to light the bonfire, as they said; others had guns and pistols, some of them charged, and some of them not; some had bagnets and ould rusty swords, pitchforks, and so on. Myself had nothing in my hand but the flail I was thrashing wid that day—and, to tell the thruth, the divil a step I would have gone with them, only for fraid of my health; for, as I said a while agone, if any discovery was made afterwards, them that promised to go and turned tail would be marked as the informers. Neither was I so blind but I could see that there war plenty there that would stay away if they durst.

"Well, we went on till we came to a little dark corner below the house, where we met, and held a council of war upon what we should do. Collier and the other strangers from behind the mountains war to go first, and the rest war to stand round the house at a distance — he carried the lantern, a bagnet, and a horse pistol; and half a dozen more war to bring over bottles of straw from Vengeance's own hagyard, to hould up to the thatch. It's all past and gone now—but three of the Reillys were desperate against Vesey that night, particularly one of them that he had shot about a year and a half before—that is, peppered two of the right-hand fingers off of him one night in a scuffle as Vesey came home from an Orange-lodge. Well, all went on purty fair; we had got as far as the outhouses, where we stopped to see if we could hear any noise, but all was quiet as you plase.

"'Now, Vengeance,' says Reilly, swearing a terrible oath out of him—'you murdering Orange villain, you're going to get your pay,' says he.

"'Ay,' says M'Guigan, 'what he often threatened to others, he'll soon meet himself, plase God. Come, boys,' says he, 'bring the straw and light it, and just lay it up, my darlings, nicely to the thatch here, and ye'll see what a glorious bonfire we'll have of the black Orange villain's blankets in less than no time.'

40

"Some of us could hardly stand this. 'Stop, boys,' cried one of Dan Slevin's sons—'stop; Vengeance is bad enough, but his wife and childher never offended us—we'll not burn the place.'

"'No,' said others, spaking out when they heard anybody at all having courage to do so—'it's too bad, boys, to burn the place; for if we do,' says they, 'some of the innocent may be burned before they get out from the house, or even before they waken out of their sleep.'

"'Knock at the door first,' says Slevin, 'and bring Vengeance out; let us cut the ears off his head, and lave him.'

"'Damn him!' says another, 'let us not take the vagabone's life; it's enough to take the ears from him, and to give him a prod or two of a bagnet on the ribs; but don't kill him.'

"'Well, well,' says Reilly, 'let us knock at the door, and get himself and the family out,' says he, 'and then we'll see what can be done wid him.'

"'Tattheration to me,' says the big Longford fellow, 'if he had sarved me, Reilly, as he did you, but I'd roast him in the flames of his own house,' says he.

"'I'd have you to know,' says Slevin, 'that you have no command here, Collier. I'm captain at the present time,' says he, 'and more nor what I wish shall not be done. Go over,' says he to the black faces, 'and rap him up.'

"Accordingly, they began to knock at the door, commanding Vengeance to get up and come out to them.

"'Come, Vengeance,' says Collier, 'put on you, my good fellow, and come out till two or three of your neighbours, that wish you well, gets a sight of your purty face, you babe of grace!'

"'Who are you that wants me at all?' says Vengeance from within.

"'Come out first,' says Collier—'a few friends that has a crow to pluck with you. Walk out, *avourneen*; or if you'd rather be roasted alive, why, you may stay where you are,' says he.

"'Gentlemen,' says Vengeance, 'I have never, to my knowledge, offinded any of you; and I hope you won't be so cruel as to take an industrious, hard-working man from his family, in the clouds of the night, to do him an injury. Go home, gentlemen, in the name of God, and let me and mine alone. You're all mighty dacent gentlemen, you know, and I'm determined never to make or meddle with any of you. Sure, I know right well it's purtecting me you would be, dacent gentlemen. But I don't think there's any of my neighbours there, or they wouldn't stand by and see me injured.'

" 'Thrue for you, *avick*,' says they, giving at the same time a terrible pattherrara agin the door with two or three big stones.

" 'Stop, stop!' says Vengeance, 'don't break the door, and I'll open it. I know you're merciful, dacent gentlemen—I know you're merciful.'

" So the thief came and unbarred it quietly, and the next minute about a dozen of them that war within the house let slap at us. As God would have had it, the crowd didn't happen to be fornenst the door, or numbers of them would have been shot; and the night was dark, too, which was in our favour. The first volley was scarcely over when there was another slap from the outhouses; and, after that, another from the gardens; and, after that, to be sure, we took to our scrapers. Several of them were badly wounded; but as for Collier, he was shot dead, and M'Guigan was taken prisoner, with five more, on the spot. There never was such a chase as we got; and only that they thought there was more of us in it, they might have tuck most of us prisoners.

" 'Fly, boys!' says M'Guigan, as soon as they fired out of the house—'we've been sould,' says he, 'but I'll die game, anyhow'—and so he did, poor fellow; for although he and the other four war transported, one of them never sould the pass or stagged. Not but that they might have done it, for all that; only that there was a whisper sent to them that if they did, a single sowl belonging to one of them wouldn't be left living. The M'Guigans were cousins of Denis Kelly's, that's now laid out there above.

" From the time this tuck place till after the 'sizes, there wasn't a stir among them on any side; but when they war over, the boys began to prepare. Denis—heavens be his bed —was there in his glory. This was in the spring 'sizes, and the

42

May fair soon followed. Ah! that was the bloody sight, I'm tould—for I wasn't at it—atween the Orangemen and them. The Ribbonmen war bate, though, but not till after there was a desperate fight on both sides. I was tould that Denis Kelly that day knocked down five-and-twenty men in about three-quarters of an hour; and only that long John Grimes hot him a *polthoge* on the sconce with the butt-end of the gun, it was thought the Orangemen would be beat. That blow broke his skull, and was the manes of his death. He was carried home senseless."

"Well, Lachlin," said my brother, "if you didn't see it, I did. I happened to be looking out of John Carson's upper window; for it wasn't altogether safe to contemplate it within reach of the missiles. It was certainly a dreadful and a barbarous sight. You have often observed the calm, gloomy silence that precedes a thunderstorm; and had you been there that day you might have seen it illustrated in a scene much more awful. The thick living mass of people extended from the corner-house, nearly a quarter of a mile, at this end of the town, up to the parsonage on the other side. During the early part of the day every kind of business was carried on in a hurry and an impatience which denoted the little chance they knew there would be for transacting it in the evening.

"Up to the hour of four o'clock the fair was unusually quiet, and, on the whole, presented nothing in any way remarkable; but after that hour you might observe the busy stir and hum of the mass settling down into a deep, brooding, portentous silence, that was absolutely fearful. The females, with dismay and terror pictured in their faces, hurried home; and in various instances you might see mothers, and wives, and sisters clinging about the sons, husbands, and brothers, attempting to drag them by main force from the danger which they knew impended over them. In this they seldom succeeded; for the person so urged was usually compelled to tear himself from them by superior strength.

"The pedlars, and basket-women, and such as had tables and standings erected in the streets, commenced removing them with all possible haste. The shopkeepers and other inhabitants of the town put up their shutters, in order to secure their windows from being shattered. Strangers who were compelled to stop in town that night, took shelter in the inns and other houses of entertainment where they lodged; so that about five o'clock the street was completely clear and free for action.

"Hitherto there was not a stroke—the scene became even more silent and gloomy, although the moral darkness of their ill-suppressed passions was strongly contrasted with the splendour of the sun, that poured down a tide of golden light upon the multitude. This contrast between the natural brightness of the evening and the internal gloom of their hearts, as the beams of the sun rested upon the ever-moving crowd, would, to any man who knew the impetuosity with which the spirit of religious hatred was soon to rage among them, produce novel and singular sensations. For, after all, Toby, there is a mysterious connection between natural and moral things, which often invests both nature and sentiment with a feeling that certainly would not come home to our hearts if such a connection did not exist. A rose-tree beside a grave will lead us from sentiment to reflection; and any other association where a painful or melancholy thought is clothed with a garb of joy or pleasure, will strike us more deeply in proportion as the contrast is strong. On seeing the sun or moon struggling through the darkness of surrounding clouds, I confess, although you may smile, that I feel for the moment a diminution of enjoyment—something taken, as it were, from the sum of my happiness.

"Ere the quarrel commenced you might see a dark and hateful glare scowling from the countenances of the two parties as they viewed and approached each other in the street—the eye was set in deadly animosity, and the face marked with an ireful paleness, occasioned at once by revenge and apprehension. Groups were silently hurrying with an eager and energetic step to their places of rendezvous, grasping their weapons more closely, or grinding their teeth in the impatience of their fury. The veterans on each side were surrounded by their respective followers, anxious to act under their direction; and the very boys seemed to be animated with a martial spirit much more eager than that of those who had greater experience in party quarrels.

44

"Jem Finigan's public-house was the headquarters and rallying-point of the Ribbonmen; the Orangemen assembled in that of Joe Sherlock, the master of an Orange-lodge. About six o'clock the crowd in the street began gradually to fall off to the opposite ends of the town—the Roman Catholics towards the north, the Protestants towards the south. Carson's window, from which I was observing their motions, was exactly half-way between them, so that I had a distinct view of both. At this moment I noticed Denis Kelly coming forward from the closely condensed mass formed by the Ribbonmen; he advanced with his cravat off, to the middle of the vacant space between the parties, holding a fine oak cudgel in his hand. He then stopped, and addressing the Orangemen, said—

"'Where's Vengeance and his crew now? Is there any single Orange villain among you that dare come down and meet me here like a man? Is John Grimes there? for if he is, before we begin to take you out of a face—to hunt you altogether out of the town, ye Orange villains—I would be glad that he'd step down to Denis Kelly here for two or three minutes—I'll not keep him longer.'

"There was now a stir and a murmur among the Orangemen, as if a rush was about to take place towards Denis; but Grimes, whom I saw endeavouring to curb them in, left the crowd and advanced towards him.

"At this moment an instinctive movement among both masses took place; so that when Grimes had come within a few yards of Kelly, both parties were within two or three perches of them. Kelly was standing apparently off his guard, with one hand thrust carelessly into the breast of his waistcoat, and the cudgel in the other; but his eye was fixed calmly upon Grimes as he approached. They were both powerful, fine men—brawny, vigorous, and active. Grimes had somewhat the advantage of the other in height; he also fought with his left hand, from which circumstance he was nicknamed *Kitthogue*. He was a man of a dark, stern-looking countenance; and the tones of his voice were deep, sullen, and of appalling strength.

"As they approached each other, the windows on each side of the street were crowded; but there was not a breath to be heard in any direction, nor from either party. As for myself, my heart palpitated with anxiety. What they might have felt, I do not know; but they must both have experienced considerable apprehension; for as they were the champions of their respective parties, and had never before met in single encounter, their characters depended on the issue of the contest.

"'Well, Grimes,' said Denis, 'sure, I've often wished for this same meetin', man, betune myself and you; I have what you're going to get in for you this long time; but you'll get it now, *avick*, plase God.'

"'It was not to scould I came, you Popish, ribly rascal,' replied Grimes, 'but to give you what you're long——'

"Ere the word had been out of his mouth, however, Kelly sprung over to him; and making a feint, as if he intended to lay the stick on his ribs, he swung it past without touching him, and bringing it round his own head like lightning, made it tell with a powerful back-stroke right on Grimes's temple, and in an instant his own face was sprinkled with the blood which sprung from the wound. Grimes staggered forward towards his antagonist; seeing which, Kelly sprung back, and was again meeting him with full force, when Grimes, turning a little, clutched Kelly's stick in his right hand, and being left-handed himself, ere the other could wrench the cudgel from him, he gave him a terrible blow upon the back part of the head, which laid Kelly in the dust.

"There was then a deafening shout from the Orange party; and Grimes stood until Kelly should be in the act of rising, ready then to give him another blow. The coolness and generalship of Kelly, however, were here very remarkable; for when he was just getting to his feet, 'Look at your party coming down upon me!' he exclaimed to Grimes, who turned round to order them back, and in the interim Kelly was upon his legs.

"I was surprised at the coolness of both men; for Grimes was by no means inflated with the boisterous triumph of his party, nor did Denis get into a blind rage on being knocked down. They approached again, their eyes kindled into savage fury, tamed down into the wariness of experienced combatants; for a short time they stood eyeing each other, as if calculating upon the contingent advantages of attack or defence. This was a moment of great interest; for as their huge and powerful frames stood out in opposition, strung and dilated by passion and the energy of contest, no judgment, however experienced, could venture to anticipate the result of the battle, or name the person likely to be victorious. Indeed, it was surprising how the natural sagacity of these men threw their movements into scientific form and elegance. Kelly raised his cudgel, and placed it transversely in the air between himself and his opponent; Grimes instantly placed his against it—both weapons thus forming a St. Andrew's cross—whilst the men themselves stood foot to foot, calm and collected. Nothing could be finer than their proportions, nor superior to their respective attitudes : their broad chests were in a line ; their thick, well-set necks laid a little back, as were their bodies—without, however, losing their balance ; and their fierce but calm features grimly but placidly scowling at each other, like men who were prepared for the onset.

"At length Kelly made an attempt to repeat his former feint with variations ; for whereas he had sent the first blow to Grimes's right temple, he took measures now to reach the left. His action was rapid, but equally quick was the eye of his antagonist, whose cudgel was up in ready guard to meet the blow. It met it ; and with such surprising power was it sent and opposed that both cudgels, on meeting, bent across each other into curves. An involuntary huzza followed this from their respective parties—not so much on account of the skill displayed by the combatants, as in admiration of their cudgels, and of the judgment with which they must have been selected. In fact, it was the staves rather than the men that were praised ; and certainly the former did their duty. In a moment their *shillelaghs* were across each other once more, and the men resumed their former attitudes. Their savage determination, their kindled eyes, the blood which disfigured the face of Grimes, and begrimed also the countenance of his antagonist into a deeper expression of ferocity, occasioned many a cowardly heart to shrink from the sight. There they stood, gory and stern, ready for the next onset. It was first made by Grimes, who tried to practise

47

on Kelly the feint which Kelly had before practised on him. Denis, after his usual manner, caught the blow in his open hand, and clutched the staff with an intention of holding it until he might visit Grimes—now apparently unguarded—with a levelling blow; but Grimes's effort to wrest the cudgel from his grasp drew all Kelly's strength to that quarter, and prevented him from availing himself of the other's defence-less attitude. A trial of muscular power ensued, and their enormous bodily strength was exhibited in the stiff tug for victory. Kelly's address prevailed; for while Grimes pulled against him with all his collected vigour, the former suddenly let go his hold, and the latter, having lost his balance, staggered back. Lightning could not be more quick than the action of Kelly, as, with tremendous force, his cudgel rung on the unprotected head of Grimes, who fell, or rather was shot to the ground, as if some superior power had dashed him against it; and there he lay for a short time, quivering under the blow he had received.

"A peal of triumph now arose from Kelly's party; but Kelly himself, placing his arms akimbo, stood calmly over his enemy, awaiting his return to the conflict. For nearly five minutes he stood in this attitude, during which time Grimes did not stir; at length Kelly stooped a little, and peering closely into his face, exclaimed—

"'Why, then, is it acting you are? Anyhow, I wouldn't put it past you, you cunning vagabone—'tis lying to take breath he is. Get up, man; I'd scorn to touch you till you're on your legs—not all as one, for, sure, it's yourself would show me no such forbearance. Up with you, man alive; I've none of your own thrachery in me. I'll not rise my cudgel till you're on your guard.'

"There was an expression of disdain mingled with a glow of honest, manly generosity on his countenance as he spoke, which made him at once the favourite with such spectators as were not connected with either of the parties. Grimes arose; and it was evident that Kelly's generosity deepened his resentment more than the blow which had sent him so rapidly to the ground. However, he was still cool, but his brows knit, his eye flashed with double fierceness, and his complexion settled into a dark-blue shade, which gave to his whole visage an expression fearfully ferocious. Kelly hailed this as the first appearance of passion; his brow expanded as the other approached, and a dash of confidence, if not of triumph, softened in some degree the sternness of his features.

"With caution they encountered again, each collected for a spring, their eyes gleaming at each other like those of tigers. Grimes made a motion as if he would have struck Kelly with his fist; and as the latter threw up his guard against the blow, he received a stroke from Grimes's cudgel on the under part of the right arm. This had been directed at his elbow, with an intention of rendering the arm powerless; it fell short, however, yet was sufficient to relax the grasp which Kelly held of his weapon. Had Kelly been a novice, this stratagem alone would have soon vanquished him; his address, however, was fully equal to that of his antagonist. The staff dropped instantly from his grasp, but a stout thong of black polished leather, with a shining tassel at the end of it, had bound it securely to his massive wrist; the cudgel, therefore, only dangled from his arm, and did not, as the other expected, fall to the ground, or put Denis to the necessity of stooping for it—Grimes's object being to have struck him in that attitude.

"A flash of indignation now shot from Kelly's eye, and with the speed of lightning he sprung within Grimes's weapon, determined to wrest it from him. The grapple that ensued was gigantic. In a moment Grimes's staff was parallel with the horizon between them, clutched in the powerful grasp of both. They stood exactly opposite, and rather close to each other; their arms sometimes stretched out stiff and at full length, again contracted, until their faces, glowing and distorted by the energy of the contest, were drawn almost together. Sometimes the prevailing strength of one would raise the staff slowly, and with gradually developed power, up in a perpendicular position; again, the reaction of opposing strength would strain it back, and sway the weighty frame of the antagonist, crouched and set into desperate resistance, along with it; whilst the hard pebbles under their feet were crumbled into powder, and the very street itself furrowed into gravel by the shock of their

49

opposing strength. Indeed, so well matched a pair never met in contest; their strength, their wind, their activity, and their natural science appeared to be perfectly equal.

"At length, by a tremendous effort, Kelly got the staff twisted nearly out of Grimes's hand, and a short shout, half encouraging, half indignant, came from Grimes's party. This added shame to his other passions, and threw an impulse of almost superhuman strength into him: he recovered his advantage, but nothing more; they twisted—they heaved their great frames against each other—they struggled— their action became rapid—they swayed each other this way and that—their eyes like fire, their teeth locked, and their nostrils dilated. Sometimes they twined about each other like serpents, and twirled round with such rapidity that it was impossible to distinguish them; sometimes, when a pull of more than ordinary power took place, they seemed to cling together almost without motion, bending down until their heads nearly touched the ground, their cracking joints seeming to stretch by the effort, and the muscles of their limbs standing out from the flesh, strung in amazing tension.

"In this attitude were they, when Denis, with the eye of a hawk, spied a disadvantage in Grimes's position; he wheeled round, placed his broad shoulder against the shaggy breast of the other, and giving him what is called an 'inside crook,' strained him, despite of every effort, until he fairly got him on his shoulder, and off the point of resistance. There was a cry of alarm from the windows, particularly from the females, as Grimes's huge body was swung over Kelly's shoulder, until it came down in a crash upon the hard gravel of the street, while Denis stood in triumph, with his enemy's staff in his hand. A loud huzza followed this from all present, except the Orangemen, who stood bristling with fury and shame for the temporary defeat of their champion.

"Denis again had his enemy at his mercy, but he scorned to use his advantage ungenerously; he went over, and placing the staff in his hands—for the other had got to his legs—retrograded to his place, and desired Grimes to defend himself.

50

"After considerable manœuvring on both sides, Denis, who appeared to be the more active of the two, got an open on his antagonist, and by a powerful blow upon Grimes's ear sent him to the ground with amazing force. I never saw such a blow given by mortal: the end of the cudgel came exactly upon the ear, and as Grimes went down, the blood spurted out of his mouth and nostrils; he then kicked convulsively several times as he lay upon the ground, and that moment I really thought he would never have breathed more.

"The shout was again raised by the Ribbonmen, who threw up their hats, and bounded from the ground with the most vehement exultation. Both parties then waited to give Grimes time to rise and renew the battle; but he appeared perfectly contented to remain where he was, for there appeared no signs of life or motion in him.

"'Have you got your gruel, boy?' said Kelly, going over to where he lay. 'Well, you met Denis Kelly at last, didn't you? and there you lie; but, plase God, the most of your sort will soon lie in the same state. Come, boys,' said Kelly, addressing his own party; 'now for bloody Vengeance and his crew, that thransported the M'Guigans and the Caffries, and murdered Collier. Now, boys, have at the murderers, and let us have satisfaction for all!'

"A mutual rush instantly took place; but ere the Orangemen came down to where Grimes lay, Kelly had taken his staff and handed it to one of his own party. It is impossible to describe the scene that ensued. The noise of the blows, the shouting, the yelling, the groans, the scalped heads and gory visages gave both to the eye and the ear an impression that could not easily be forgotten. The battle was obstinately maintained on both sides for nearly an hour, and with a skill of manœuvring, attack, and retreat that was astonishing.

"Both parties arranged themselves against each other, forming something like two lines of battle, and these extended along the town nearly from one end to the other. It was curious to remark the difference in the persons and appearances of the combatants. In the Orange line the men were taller and of more powerful frames; but the Ribbonmen were more hardy, active, and courageous. Man to man,

51

notwithstanding their superior bodily strength, the Orangemen could never fight the others; the former depend too much upon their fire and side arms, but they are by no means so well trained to the use of the cudgel as their enemies. In the district where the scene of this fight is laid, the Catholics generally inhabit the mountainous part of the country, to which, when the civil feuds of worse times prevailed, they had been driven at the point of the bayonet; the Protestants and Presbyterians, on the other hand, who came in upon their possessions, occupy the richer and more fertile tracts of the land, living, of course, more wealthily, with less labour, and on better food. The characteristic features produced by these causes are such as might be expected—the Catholic being, like his soil, hardy, thin, and capable of bearing all weathers; and the Protestants, larger, softer, and more inactive.

"Their advance to the first onset was far different from a faction fight. There existed a silence here that powerfully evinced the inextinguishable animosity with which they encountered. For some time they fought in two compact bodies, that remained unbroken so long as the chances of victory were doubtful. Men went down, and were up, and went down in all directions with uncommon rapidity; and as the weighty phalanx of Orangemen stood out against the nimble line of their mountain adversaries, the intrepid spirit of the latter, and their surprising skill and activity, soon gave symptoms of a gradual superiority in the conflict. In the course of about half an hour the Orange party began to give way in the northern end of the town; and as their opponents pressed them warmly and with unsparing hand, the heavy mass formed by their numbers began to break, and this decomposition ran up their line, until in a short time they were thrown into utter confusion. They now fought in detached parties; but these subordinate conflicts, though shorter in duration than the shock of the general battle, were much more inhuman and destructive; for whenever any particular gang succeeded in putting their adversaries to flight, they usually ran to the assistance of their friends in the nearest fight — by which means they often fought three to one.

"There lived a short distance out of the town a man nicknamed Jemmy *Boccagh*, on account of his lameness—he was also sometimes called 'Hip-an'-go-constant'—who fell the first victim to party spirit. He had got arms on seeing his friends likely to be defeated, and had the hardihood to follow, with charged bayonet, a few Ribbonmen, whom he attempted to intercept as they fled from a large number of their enemies who had got them separated from their comrades. *Boccagh* ran across a field, in order to get before them on the road, and was in the act of climbing a ditch, when one of them, who carried a spade-shaft, struck him a blow on the head which put an end to his existence.

"This circumstance imparted, of course, fiercer hatred to both parties—triumph inspiring the one, a thirst for vengeance nerving the other. Kelly inflicted tremendous punishment in every direction; for scarcely a blow fell from him which did not bring a man to the ground. It absolutely resembled a military engagement, for the number of combatants amounted at least to two thousand men. In many places the street was covered with small pools and clots of blood which flowed from those who lay insensible; while others were borne away bleeding, groaning, or staggering, having been battered into a total unconsciousness of the scene about them.

"At length the Orangemen gave way, and their enemies, yelling with madness and revenge, began to beat them with unrestrained fury. The former, finding that they could not resist the impetuous tide which burst upon them, fled back past the church, and stopped not until they had reached an elevation, on which lay two or three heaps of stones that had been collected for the purpose of paving the streets. Here they made a stand, and commenced a vigorous discharge of them against their pursuers. This checked the latter; and the others, seeing them hesitate, and likely to retreat from the missiles, pelted them with such effect that the tables became turned, and the Ribbonmen made a speedy flight back into the town.

"In the meantime several Orangemen had gone into Sherlock's, where a considerable number of arms had been deposited, with an intention of resorting to them in case of a defeat at the cudgels. These now came out, and met the Ribbonmen on their flight from those who were pelting them with the stones. A dreadful scene ensued. The Ribbonmen, who had the advantage in numbers, finding themselves intercepted before by those who had arms, and pursued behind by those who had recourse to the stones, fought with uncommon bravery and desperation. Kelly, who was furious, but still collected and decisive, shouted out in Irish, lest the opposite party might understand him, 'Let every two men seize upon one of those who have the arms.'

"This was attempted, and effected with partial success; and I have no doubt but the Orangemen would have been ultimately beaten and deprived of their weapons, were it not that many of them who had got their pistols out of Sherlock's discharged them among their enemies, and wounded several. The Catholics could not stand this; but wishing to retaliate as effectually as possible, lifted stones wherever they could find them, and kept up the fight at a distance as they retreated. On both sides, wherever a solitary foe was caught straggling from the rest, he was instantly punished.

"It was just about this time that I saw Kelly engaged with two men, whom he kept at bay with great ease—retrograding, however, as he fought, towards his own party. Grimes, who had some time before this recovered and joined the fight once more, was returning, after having pursued several of the Ribbonmen past the market-house, where he spied Kelly thus engaged. With a volunteer gun in his hand, and furious with the degradation of his former defeat, he ran over and struck him with the butt-end of it upon the temple, and Denis fell. When the stroke was given, an involuntary cry of 'Murder—foul, foul!' burst from those who looked on from the windows, and long John Steele, Grimes's father-in-law, in indignation raised his cudgel to knock him down for this treacherous and malignant blow; but a person out of Neal Cassidy's back-yard hurled a round stone, about six pounds in weight, at Grimes's head, that felled him to the earth, leaving him as insensible, and nearly in as dangerous a state, as Kelly, for his jaw was broken.

" By this time the Catholics had retreated out of the town, and Denis might probably have received more punishment had those who were returning from the pursuit recognised him; but James Wilson, seeing the dangerous situation in which he lay, came out, and, with the assistance of his servant-man, brought him into his own house. When the Orangemen had driven their adversaries off the field, they commenced the most hideous yellings through the streets—got music and played party tunes—offered any money for the face of a Papist; and any of that religion who were so unfortunate as to make their appearance were beaten in the most relentless manner. It was precisely the same thing on the part of the Ribbonmen: if a Protestant, but, above all, an Orangeman, came in their way, he was sure to be treated with barbarity—for the retaliation on either side was dreadfully unjust, the innocent suffering as well as the guilty. Leaving the window, I found Kelly in a bad state below stairs.

" ' What's to be done ?' said I to Wilson.

" ' I know not,' replied he, 'except I put him between us on my jaunting-car and drive him home.'

" This appeared decidedly the best plan we could adopt; so, after putting to the horse, we placed him on the car, sitting one on each side of him, and in this manner left him at his own house."

" Did you run no risk," said I, " in going among Kelly's friends whilst they were under the influence of party feeling and exasperated passion ? "

" No," said he; " we had rendered many of them acts of kindness, and had never exhibited any spirit but a friendly one towards them; and such individuals, but only such, might walk through a crowd of enraged Catholics or Protestants quite unmolested.

" The next morning Kelly's landlord and two magistrates were at his house; but he lay like a log, without sense or motion. Whilst they were there the surgeon arrived, and after examining his head, declared that the skull was fractured. During that and the following day the house was surrounded by crowds, anxious to know his state; and nothing might be heard amongst most of them but loud and undisguised expressions of the most ample revenge. .The wife was frantic, and, on seeing me, hid her face in her hands, exclaiming—

" 'Ah, sir, I knew it would come to this; and you, too, tould him the same thing. My curse and God's curse on it for quarrelling! Will it never stop in the counthry till they rise some time and murdher one another out of the face!'

" As soon as the swelling in his head was reduced, the surgeon performed the operation of trepanning, and thereby saved his life; but his strength and intellect were gone, and he just lingered for four months, a feeble, drivelling simpleton, until, in consequence of a cold, which produced inflammation in the brain, he died, as hundreds have died, the victim of party spirit."

Such was the account which I heard of my old schoolfellow Denis Kelly; and, indeed, when I reflected upon the nature of the education he received, I could not but admit that the consequences were such as might naturally be expected to result from it.

The next morning a relation of Mrs. Kelly's came down to my brother, hoping that, as they wished to have as decent a funeral as possible, he would be so kind as to attend it.

" *Musha*, God knows, sir," said the man, " it's poor Denis —heavens be his bed—that had the regard and reverence for every one, young and ould, of your father's family; and it's himself that would be the proud man, if he was living, to see you, sir, riding after his coffin."

" Well," said my brother, " let Mrs. Kelly know that I shall certainly attend, and so will my brother, here, who has come to pay me a visit. Why, I believe, Tom, you forget him!"

" Your brother, sir! Is it Masther Toby, that used to cudgel the half of the counthry when he was at school? Gad's my life, Masther Toby (I was now about thirty-six), but it's your four quarters, sure enough! *Arrah*, thin, sir, who'd think it—you're grown so full and stout — but, faix, you'd always the bone in you! Ah, Masther Toby!" said he, " he's lying cowld this morning that would be the happy man to lay his eyes wanst more upon you. Many an' many's the winther's evening did he spind talking about the time when you and he were *bouchals* together, and of the pranks

56

you played at school, but especially of the time you both leathered the four Grogans, and tuck the apples from them —my poor fellow!—and now to be stretched a corpse, lavin' his poor widdy and childher behind him!"

I accordingly expressed my sorrow for Denis's death, which, indeed, I sincerely regretted, for he possessed materials for an excellent character, had not all that was amiable and good in him been permitted to run wild.

As soon as my trunk and travelling-bag had been brought from the inn where I had left them the preceding night, we got our horses, and as we wished to show particular respect to Denis's remains, rode up, with some of our friends, to the house. When we approached, there were large crowds of the country-people before the door of his well-thatched and re-spectable-looking dwelling, which had three chimneys, and a set of sash-windows, clean and well glazed. On our arrival I was soon recognised and surrounded by numbers of those to whom I had formerly been known, who received and welcomed me with a warmth of kindness and sincerity which it would be in vain to look for among the peasantry of any other nation.

Indeed, I have uniformly observed that when no religious or political feeling influences the heart and principles of an Irish peasant, he is singularly sincere and faithful in his attach-ments, and has always a bias to the generous and the dis-interested. To my own knowledge, circumstances frequently occur in which the ebullition of party spirit is altogether temporary, subsiding after the cause that produced it has passed away, and leaving the kind peasant to the naturally affectionate and generous impulses of his character. But poor Paddy, unfortunately, is as combustible a material in politics or religion as in fighting—thinking it his duty to take the weak [1] side, without any other consideration than because it is the weak side.

[1] A gentleman once told me an anecdote of which he was an eye-witness. Some peasants belonging to opposite factions had met under peculiar circumstances ; there were, however, two on one side, and four on the other. In this case there was likely to be no fight ; but, in order to balance the number, one of the more numerous party joined the weak side—" Bekase, boys, it would be a burnin' shame, so it would, for four to lick two ; and, except I join them, by the powers, there's no chance of there being a bit of sport or a row, at all, at all !"

When we entered the house I was almost suffocated with the strong fumes of tobacco-smoke, snuff, and whisky; and as I had been an old schoolfellow of Denis's, my appearance was the signal for a general burst of grief among his relations, in which the more distant friends and neighbours of the deceased joined, to keep up the *keening*.

I have often, indeed always, felt that there is something extremely touching in the Irish cry; in fact, that it breathes the very spirit of wild and natural sorrow. The Irish peasantry, whenever a death takes place, are exceedingly happy in seizing upon any contingent circumstances that may occur, and making them subservient to the excitement of grief for the departed, or the exultation and praise of his character and virtues. My entrance was a proof of this—I had scarcely advanced to the middle of the floor, when my intimacy with the deceased, our boyish sports, and even our quarrels, were adverted to with a natural eloquence and pathos that, in spite of my firmness, occasioned me to feel the prevailing sorrow. They spoke, or chanted mournfully, in Irish; but the substance of what they said was as follows :—

"Oh, Denis, Denis, *avourneen!* you're lying low this morning of sorrow!—lying low, are you, and does not know who it is (alluding to me) that is standing over you, weeping for the days you spent together in your youth ! It's yourself, *acushla agus asthore machree* (the pulse and beloved of my heart), that would stretch out the right hand warmly to welcome him to the place of his birth, where you had both been so often happy about the green hills and valleys with each other ! He's here now, standing over you; and it's he, of all his family, kind and respectable as they are, that was your own favourite, Denis, *avourneen dheelish!* He alone was the companion that you loved !—with no other could you be happy ! For him did you fight when he wanted a friend in your young quarrels ! and if you had a dispute with him, were not you sorry for it? Are you not now stretched in death before him, and will he not forgive you?"

All this was uttered, of course, extemporaneously, and without the least preparation. They then passed on to an enumeration of his virtues as a father, a husband, son, and brother—specified his worth as he stood related to

58

society in general, and his kindness as a neighbour and a friend.

An occurrence now took place which may serve in some measure to throw light upon many of the atrocities and outrages which take place in Ireland. Before I mention it, however, I think it necessary to make a few observations relative to it. I am convinced that those who are intimately acquainted with the Irish peasantry will grant that there is not on the earth a class of people in whom the domestic affections of blood-relationship are so pure, strong, and sacred. The birth of a child will occasion a poor man to break in upon the money set apart for his landlord, in order to keep the christening among his friends and neighbours with due festivity. A marriage exhibits a spirit of joy, an exuberance of happiness and delight, to be found only in the Green Island; and the death of a member of a family is attended with a sincerity of grief scarcely to be expected from men so much the creatures of the more mirthful feelings. In fact, their sorrow is a solecism in humanity—at once deep and loud—mingled up, even in its greatest paroxysms, with a laughter-loving spirit. It is impossible that an Irishman sunk in the lowest depths of affliction could permit his grief to flow in all the sad solemnity of affliction even for a day, without some glimpse of his natural humour throwing a faint and rapid light over the gloom within him. No; there is an amalgamation of sentiments in his mind which, as I said before, would puzzle any philosopher to account for. Yet it would be wrong to say, though his grief has something of an unsettled and ludicrous character about it, that he is incapable of the most subtle and delicate shades of sentiment, or the deepest and most desolating intensity of sorrow. But he laughs off those heavy vapours which hang about the moral constitution of the people of other nations, giving them a morbid habit which leaves them neither strength nor firmness to resist calamity, which they feel less keenly than an Irishman, exactly as a healthy man will feel the pangs of death with more acuteness than one who is wasted away by debility and decay. Let any man witness an emigration, and he will satisfy himself that this is true. I am convinced that Goldsmith's inimitable description of one in his "Deserted

59

Village " was a picture drawn from actual observation. Let him observe the emigrant as he crosses the Atlantic, and he will find, although he joins the jest, and the laugh, and the song, that he will seek a silent corner or a silent hour to indulge the sorrow which he still feels for the friends, the companions, and the native fields that he has left behind him. This constitution of mind is beneficial; the Irishman seldom or never hangs himself, because he is capable of too much real feeling to permit himself to become the slave of that which is factitious. There is no void in his affections or sentiments which a morbid and depraved sensibility could occupy; but his feelings, of what character soever they may be, are strong, because they are fresh and healthy. For this reason I maintain that when the domestic affections come under the influence of either grief or joy the peasantry of no nation are capable of feeling so deeply. Even on the ordinary occasions of death, sorrow, though it alternates with mirth and cheerfulness in a manner peculiar to themselves, lingers long in the unseen recesses of domestic life; any hand, therefore, whether by law or violence, that plants a wound *here*, will suffer to the death.

When my brother and I entered the house the body had just been put into the coffin; and it is usual after this takes place, and before it is nailed down, for the immediate relatives of the family to embrace the deceased, and take their last look and farewell of his remains. In the present instance the children were brought over, one by one, to perform that trying and melancholy ceremony. The first was an infant on the breast, whose little innocent mouth was held down to that of its dead father; the babe smiled upon his still and solemn features, and would have played with his grave-clothes, but that the murmur of unfeigned sorrow which burst from all present occasioned it to be removed. The next was a fine little girl of three or four years, who inquired where they were going to bring her daddy, and asked if he would not soon come back to her.

" My daddy's sleepin' a long time," said the child, "but I'll waken him till he sings me 'Peggy Slevin.' I like my daddy best, bekase I sleep wid him ; and he brings me good things from the fair—he bought me this ribbon," said she, pointing to a ribbon which he had purchased for her.

The rest of the children were sensible of their loss, and truly it was a distressing scene. His eldest son and daughter, the former about fourteen, the latter about two years older, lay on the coffin, kissing his lips, and were with difficulty torn away from it.

"Oh!" said the boy, "he is going from us, and night or day we will never see him or hear of him more! Oh! father —father—is that the last sight we are ever to see of your face? Why, father dear, did you die, and leave us for ever— for ever? Wasn't your heart good to us, and your words kind to us? Oh! your last smile is smiled—your last kiss given— and your last kind word spoken to your childher that you loved, and that loved you as we did. Father, core of my heart, are you gone for ever, and your voice departed? Oh! the murdherers—oh! the murdherers, the murdherers!" he exclaimed, "that killed my father; for only for them he would be still wid us—but, by the God that's over me, if I live, night or day I will not rest till I have blood for blood; nor do I care who hears it, nor if I was hanged the next minute."

As these words escaped him, a deep and awful murmur of suppressed vengeance burst from his relations. At length their sorrow became too strong to be repressed; and as it was the time to take their last embrace and look of him, they came up, and after fixing their eyes on his face in deep afflic- tion, their lips began to quiver, and their countenances became convulsed. They then burst out simultaneously into a tide of violent grief, which, after having indulged in it for some time, they checked. But the resolution of revenge was stronger than their grief, for, standing over his dead body, they repeated, almost word for word, the vow of vengeance which the son had just sworn. It was really a scene dread- fully and terribly solemn; and I could not avoid reflecting upon the mystery of nature, which can, from the deep power of domestic affection, cause to spring a determination to crime of so black a dye. Would to God that our peasantry had a clearer sense of moral and religious duties, and were not left so much as they are to the headlong impulse of an ardent temperament and an impetuous character; and would to God that the clergy who superintend their education and morals had a better knowledge of human nature!

During all this time the heart-broken widow sat beyond the coffin, looking upon what passed with a stupid sense of bereavement; and when they had all performed this last ceremony, it was found necessary to tell her that the time was come for the procession of the funeral, and that they only waited for her to take, as the rest did, her last look and embrace of her husband. When she heard this, it pierced her like an arrow: she became instantly collected, and her complexion assumed a dark sallow shade of despairing anguish, which it was an affliction even to look upon. She then stooped over the coffin, and kissed him several times, after which she ceased sobbing, and lay silently with her mouth to his.

The character of a faithful wife sorrowing for a beloved husband has that in it which compels both respect and sympathy. There was not at this moment a dry eye in the house. She still lay silent on the coffin; but as I observed that her bosom seemed not to heave as it did a little before, I was convinced that she had become insensible. I accordingly beckoned to Kelly's brother, to whom I mentioned what I had suspected; and on his going over to ascertain the truth, he found her as I had said. She was then brought to the air, and after some trouble recovered; but I recommended them to put her to bed, and not to subject her to any unnecessary anguish by a custom which was really too soul-piercing to endure. This, however, was, in her opinion, the violation of an old rite sacred to her heart and affections— she would not hear of it for an instant. Again she was helped out between her brother and brother-in-law; and after stooping down and doing as the others had done—

"Now," said she, "I will sit here, and keep him under my eye as long as I can—surely you won't blame me for it; you all know the kind husband he was to me, and the good right I have to be sorry for him! Oh!" she added, "is it thrue at all?—is he, my own Denis, the young husband of my airly love, in good arnest, dead, and going to leave me here—me, Denis, that you loved so tindherly, and our childher that your brow was never clouded against? Can I believe myself, or is it a dhrame? Denis, *avick machree! avick machree!* your hand was dreaded, and a good right it had, for it was the manly hand, that was ever and always raised in defence of them that wanted a friend; abroad, in the faction fight, against the oppressor, your name was ever feared, *acushla!*—but at home—AT HOME—where was your fellow? Denis, *achora,* do you know the lips that's spaking to you?—your young bride—your heart's light. Oh! I remimber the day you war married to me like yesterday. Oh! *avourneen,* then and since wasn't the heart of your own Honor bound up in you—yet not a word even to me. Well, *agra machree,* 'tisn't your fault; it's the first time you ever refused to spake to your own Honor. But you're dead, *avourneen,* or it wouldn't be so—you're dead before my eyes, husband of my heart, and all my hopes and happiness goes into the coffin and the grave along wid you for ever!"

All this time she was rocking herself from side to side, her complexion pale and ghastly as could be conceived. When the coffin was about to be closed, she retired until it was nailed down; after which she returned with her bonnet and cloak on her, ready to accompany it to the grave. I was astonished, for I thought she could not have walked two steps without assistance; but it was the custom, and to neglect it, I found, would have thrown the imputation of insincerity upon her grief. While they were preparing to bring the coffin out, I could hear the chat and conversation of those who were standing in crowds before the door, and occasionally a loud vacant laugh, and sometimes a volley of them, responsive to the jokes of some rustic wit, probably the same person who acted as master of the revels at the wake.

Before the coffin was finally closed, Ned Corrigan, whom I had put to flight the preceding night, came up, and repeated the *De profundis* in very strange Latin over the corpse. When this was finished, he got a jug of holy water, and after dipping his thumb in it, first made the sign of the cross upon his own forehead, and afterwards sprinkled it upon all present, giving my brother and myself an extra compliment, supposing, probably, that we stood most in need of it. When this was over, he sprinkled the corpse and the coffin in particular most profusely. He then placed two pebbles from Lough Derg, and a bit of holy candle, upon the breast of the corpse, and having said a *Pater* and *Ave*, in which he was joined by the people, he closed the lid and nailed it down.

"Ned," said his brother, "are his feet and toes loose?"

"*Musha*, but that's more than myself knows," replied Ned. "Are they, Katty?" said he, inquiring from the sister of the deceased.

"*Arrah*, to be sure, *avourneen*," answered Katty. "Div you think we would lave him to be tied that a-way when he'd be risin' out of his last bed? Wouldn't it be too bad to have his toes tied thin, *avourneen*?"

The coffin was then brought out and placed upon four chairs before the door to be keened; and in the meantime the friends and well-wishers of the deceased were brought into the room to get each a glass of whisky as a token of respect. I observed also that such as had not seen any of Kelly's relations until then, came up, and shaking hands with them, said, "I'm sorry for your loss!" This expression of condolence was uniform, and the usual reply was, "Thank you, Mat, or Jim!" with a pluck of the skirts, accompanied by a significant nod to follow. They then got a due share of whisky; and it was curious, after they came out, their faces a little flushed, and their eyes watery with the strong, ardent spirits, to hear with what heartiness and alacrity they entered into Denis's praises.

When he had been keened in the street, there being no hearse, the coffin was placed upon two handspikes which were fixed across, but parallel to each other, under it. These were borne by four men, one at the end of each, with the point of it touching his body a little below his stomach—in other parts of Ireland the coffin is borne on the shoulders, but this is more convenient and less distressing.

When we got out upon the road the funeral was of great extent, for Kelly had been highly respected. On arriving at the *merin* which bounded the land he had owned, the coffin was laid down, and a loud and wailing *keena* took place over it. It was again raised, and the funeral proceeded in a direction which I was surprised to see it take, and it was not until an acquaintance of my brother's had explained the matter that I understood the cause of it. In Ireland when a murder is perpetrated, it is usual, as the funeral proceeds to the graveyard, to bring the corpse to the house of him who committed the crime, and lay it down at his door, while the relations of the deceased kneel down, and with an appalling solemnity utter the deepest imprecations, and invoke the justice of Heaven on the head of the murderer. This, however, is usually omitted if the residence of the criminal be completely out of the line of the funeral; but if it be possible by any circuit to approach it, this dark ceremony is never omitted. In cases where the crime is doubtful or unjustly imputed, those who are thus visited come out, and laying their right hand upon the coffin, protest their innocence of the blood of the deceased, calling God to witness the truth of their asseverations; but in cases where the crime is clearly proved against the murderer, the door is either closed, the ceremony repelled by violence, or the house abandoned by the inmates until the funeral passes.

The death of Kelly, however, could not be actually, or at least directly, considered a murder, for it was probable that Grimes did not inflict the stroke with an intention of taking away his life, and, besides, Kelly survived it four months. Grimes's house was not more than fifteen perches from the road; and when the corpse was opposite the little bridle-way that led up to it, they laid it down for a moment, and the relations of Kelly surrounded it, offering up a short prayer with uncovered heads. It was then borne towards the house, whilst the keening commenced in a loud and wailing cry, accompanied with clapping of hands and every other symptom of external sorrow. But independent of their compliance with this ceremony as an old usage, there is little doubt that the appearance of anything connected with the man who certainly occasioned Kelly's death awoke a keener and more intense sorrow for his loss. The wailing was thus continued until the coffin was laid opposite Grimes's door; nor did it cease then, but, on the contrary, was renewed with louder and more bitter lamentations.

As the multitude stood compassionating the affliction of

65

the widow and orphans, it was the most impressive and solemn spectacle that could be witnessed. The very house seemed to have a condemned look; and as a single wintry breeze waved a tuft of long grass that grew on a seat of turf at the side of the door, it brought the vanity of human enmity before my mind with melancholy force. When the keening ceased, Kelly's wife, with her children, knelt, their faces towards the house of their enemy, and invoked, in the strong language of excited passion, the justice of Heaven upon the head of the man who had left her a widow, and her children fatherless. I was anxious to know if Grimes would appear to disclaim the intention of murder; but I understood that he was at market, for it happened to be market-day.

"Come out!" said the widow—"come out, and look at the sight that's here before you! Come and view your work! Lay but your hand upon the coffin, and the blood of him that you murdhered will spout, before God and these Christhen people, in your guilty face! But, oh! may the Almighty God bring this home to you! May you never lave this life, John Grimes, till worse nor has overtaken me and mine falls upon you and yours! May our curse light upon you this day—the curse, I say, of the widow and the orphans—and that your bloody hand has made us—may it blast you! May you and all belonging to you wither off the 'arth! Night and day, sleeping and waking, like snow off the ditch may you melt, until your name and your place will be disremimbered, except to be cursed by them that will hear of you and your hand of murdher! Amin, we pray God this day!—and the widow and orphans' prayer will not fall to the ground while your guilty head is above! Childher, did you all say it?"

At this moment a deep, terrific murmur, or rather ejaculation, corroborative of assent to this dreadful imprecation, pervaded the crowd in a fearful manner; their countenances darkened, their eyes gleamed, and their scowling visages stiffened into an expression of determined vengeance.

When these awful words were uttered, Grimes's wife and daughters approached the window in tears, sobbing at the same time loudly and bitterly.

"You're wrong," said the wife—"you're wrong, Widow

Kelly, in saying that my husband murdhered him!—he did not murdher him ; for when you and yours were far from him, I heard John Grimes declare, before the God who's to judge him, that he had no thought or intention of taking his life— he struck him in anger, and the blow did him an injury that was not intended. Don't curse him, Honor Kelly," said she —"don't curse him so fearfully ; but, above all, don't curse me and my innocent childher, for *we* never harmed you nor wished you ill ! *But it was this party work did it !* Oh, my God ! " she exclaimed, wringing her hands, in utter bitterness of spirit, "when will it be ended between friends and neigh- bours, that ought to live in love and kindness together, instead of fighting in this bloodthirsty manner ! "

She then wept more violently, as did her daughters.

" May God give me mercy in the last day, Mrs. Kelly, as I pity from my heart and soul you and your orphans," she continued ; " but don't curse us, for the love of God—for you know we should forgive our enemies, as we ourselves, that are the enemies of God, hope to be forgiven."

"May God forgive me, then, if I have wronged you or your husband," said the widow, softened by their distress ; " but you know that, whether he intended his life or not, the stroke he gave him has left my childher without a father, and myself dissolate. Oh, heavens above me ! " she ex- claimed, in a scream of distraction and despair, "is it possible —is it thrue—that my manly husband, the best father that ever breathed the breath of life, my own Denis, is lying dead—murdhered before my eyes ! Put your hands on my head, some of you—put your hands on my head, or it will go to pieces. Where are you, Denis—where are you, the strong of hand and the tender of heart ? Come to me, darling ; I want you in my distress. I want comfort, Denis ; and I'll take it from none but yourself, for kind was your word to me in all my afflictions ! "

All present were affected ; and, indeed, it was difficult to say whether Kelly's wife or Grimes's was more to be pitied at the moment. The affliction of the latter and of her daughters was really pitiable : their sobs were loud, and the tears streamed down their cheeks like rain. When the widow's exclamations had ceased, or rather were lost in the loud cry of sorrow which was uttered by the keeners and friends of the deceased, they, too, standing somewhat apart from the rest, joined in it bitterly ; and the solitary wail of Mrs. Grimes, differing in character from that of those who had been trained to modulate the most profound grief into strains of a melancholy nature, was particularly wild and impressive. At all events, her Christian demeanour, joined to the sincerity of her grief, appeased the enmity of many ; so true is it that a soft answer turneth away wrath. I could perceive, however, that the resentment of Kelly's male relations did not at all appear to be in any degree moderated.

The funeral again proceeded, and I remarked that whenever a strange passenger happened to meet it he always turned back and accompanied it for a short distance, after which he resumed his journey, it being considered unlucky to omit this usage on meeting a funeral. Denis's residence was not more than two miles from the churchyard, which was situated in the town where he had received the fatal blow. As soon as we had got on about the half of this way, the priest of the parish met us, and the funeral after proceeding a few perches more, turned into a green field, in the corner of which stood a table with the apparatus for saying mass spread upon it.

The coffin was then laid down once more, immediately before this temporary altar ; and the priest, after having robed himself, the wrong side of the vestments out, as is usual in the case of death, began to celebrate mass for the dead, the congregation all kneeling. When this was finished, the friends of the deceased approached the altar, and after some private conversation, the priest turned round and inquired aloud—

"Who will give offerings ? "

The people were acquainted with the manner in which this matter is conducted, and accordingly knew what to do. When the priest put the question, Denis's brother, who was a wealthy man, came forward, and laid down two guineas on the altar ; the priest took this up, and putting it on a plate, set out among the multitude, accompanied by two or three of those who were best acquainted with the inhabitants of the parish. He thus continued putting the question distinctly after each man had paid; and according as the money was laid down, those who accompanied the priest pronounced the name of the person who gave it, so that all present might hear it. This is also done to enable the friends of the deceased to know not only those who show them this mark of respect, but those who neglect it, in order that they may treat them in the same manner on similar occasions. The amount of money so received is very great; for there is a kind of emulation among the people as to who will act with most decency and spirit, that is exceedingly beneficial to the priest. In such instances the difference of religion is judiciously overlooked; for although the prayers of Protestants are declined on those occasions, yet it seems the same objection does not hold good against their money, and accordingly they pay as well as the rest. When the priest came round to where I stood, he shook hands with my brother, with whom he appeared to be on very friendly and familiar terms; he and I were then introduced to each other.

"Come," said he, with a very droll expression of countenance, shaking the plate at the same time up near my brother's nose—"come, Mr. D'Arcy, down with your offerings, if you wish to have a friend with St. Peter when you go as far as the gates; down with your money, sir, and you shall be remembered, depend upon it."

"Ah!" said my brother, pulling out a guinea, "I would with the greatest pleasure; but I fear this is not orthodox. I'm afraid it has the heretical mark upon it."

"In that case," replied his reverence, laughing heartily, "your only plan is to return it to the bosom of the Church by laying it on the plate here—it will then be within the pale, you know."

This reply produced a good deal of good-humour among that part of the crowd which immediately surrounded them— not excepting his nearest relations, who laughed heartily.

"Well," said my brother, as he laid it on the plate, "how many prayers will you offer up in my favour for this?"

"Leave that to myself," said his reverence, looking at the money—"it will be before you when you go to St. Peter."

He then held the plate out to me in a droll manner; and I

added another guinea to my brother's gift, for which I had the satisfaction of having my name called out so loud that it might be heard a quarter of a mile off.

"God bless you, sir," said the priest, "and I thank you."

"John," said I, when he left us, "I think that is a pleasant and rather a sensible man?"

"He's as jovial a soul," replied my brother, "as ever gave birth to a jest, and he sings a right good song. Many a convivial hour have he and I spent together; but, as to being a Catholic in their sense—Lord help you! At all events, he is no bigot; but, on the contrary, a liberal, and, putting religion out of the question, a kind and benevolent man."

When the offerings were all collected he returned to the altar, repeated a few additional prayers in prime style, as rapid as lightning; and after hastily shaking the holy water on the crowd, the funeral moved on. It was now two o'clock, the day clear and frosty, and the sun unusually bright for the season. During mass, many were added to those who formed the funeral train at the outset; so that when we got out upon the road the procession appeared very large. After this, few or none joined it; for it is esteemed by no means "dacent" to do so after mass, because, in that case, the matter is ascribed to an evasion of the offerings; but those whose delay has not really been occasioned by this motive make it a point to pay them at the graveyard or after the interment, and sometimes even on the following day—so jealous are the peasantry of having any degrading suspicion attached to their generosity.

The order of the funeral now was as follows: foremost the women; next to them the corpse, surrounded by the relations; the eldest son, in deep affliction, "led the coffin," as chief mourner, holding in his hand the corner of a sheet or piece of linen, fastened to the mort-cloth; after the coffin came those who were on foot, and in the rear were the equestrians. When we were a quarter of a mile from the churchyard the funeral was met by a dozen of singing boys, belonging to a chapel choir which the priest, who was fond of music, had some time before formed. They fell in, two by two, immediately behind the corpse, and commenced singing the "Requiem," or Latin hymn for the dead.

70

The scene through which we passed at this time, though not clothed with the verdure and luxuriant beauty of summer, was nevertheless marked by that solemn and decaying splendour which characterises a fine country, lit up by the melancholy light of a winter setting sun. It was therefore much more in character with the occasion. Indeed, I felt it altogether beautiful; and as the "dying day-hymn stole aloft," the dim sunbeams fell, through a vista of naked, motionless trees, upon the coffin, which was borne with a slower and more funereal pace than before, in a manner that threw a solemn and visionary light upon the whole procession. This, however, was raised to something dreadfully impressive when the long train, thus proceeding with a motion so mournful, was seen each covered with a profusion of crimson ribbons, to indicate that the corpse they bore owed his death to a deed of murder. The circumstance of the sun glancing his rays upon the coffin was not unobserved by the peasantry, who considered it as a good omen to the spirit of the departed.

As we went up the street which had been the scene of the quarrel that proved so fatal to Kelly, the coffin was again laid down on the spot where he received his death-blow; and, as was usual, the wild and melancholy *keena* was raised. My brother saw many of Grimes's friends among the spectators, but he himself was not visible. Whether Kelly's party saw them or not, we could not say; if they did, they seemed not to notice them, for no expression of revenge or indignation escaped them.

At length we entered the last receptacle of the dead. The coffin was now placed upon the shoulders of the son and brothers of the deceased, and borne round the churchyard; whilst the priest, with his stole upon him, preceded it, reading prayers for the eternal repose of the soul. Being then laid beside the grave, a *De profundis* was repeated by the priest and the mass-server; after which a portion of fresh clay, carried from the fields, was brought to his reverence, who read a prayer over it and consecrated it. This is a ceremony which is never omitted at the interment of a Roman Catholic. When it was over, the coffin was lowered into the grave, and the blessed clay shaken over it. The priest now took the shovel in his own hands, and threw in the three first shovelfuls —one in the name of the Father, one in the name of the Son, and one in the name of the Holy Ghost. The sexton then took it, and in a short time Denis Kelly was fixed for ever in his narrow bed.

While these ceremonies were going forward, the churchyard presented a characteristic picture. Beside the usual groups who straggle through the place to amuse themselves by reading the inscriptions on the tombs, you might see many individuals kneeling on particular graves, where some relation lay, for the benefit of whose soul they offered up their prayers with an attachment and devotion which one cannot but admire. Sometimes all the surviving members of the family would assemble, and repeat a "Rosary" for the same purpose. Again, you might see an unhappy woman beside a newly-made grave, giving way to lamentation and sorrow for the loss of a husband or of some beloved child. Here you might observe the "last bed" ornamented with hoops, decked in white paper, emblematic of the virgin innocence of the individual who slept below; there a little board-cross, informing you that "this monument was erected by a disconsolate husband to the memory of his beloved wife." But that which excited greatest curiosity was a sycamore tree which grew in the middle of the burying-ground.

It is necessary to inform the reader that in Ireland many of the churchyards are exclusively appropriated to the interment of Roman Catholics, and consequently no Protestant corpse would be permitted to pollute or desecrate them. This was one of them; but it appears that, by some means or other, the body of a Protestant had been interred in it—and hear the consequence! The next morning Heaven marked its disapprobation of this awful visitation by a miracle; for ere the sun rose from the east a full-grown sycamore had shot up out of the heretical grave, and stands there to this day, a monument at once of the profanation and its consequence. Crowds were looking at this tree, feeling a kind of awe, mingled with wonder, at the deed which drew down such a visible and lasting mark of God's displeasure. On the tombstones near Kelly's grave, men and women were seated, smoking tobacco to their very heart's content; for with that

72

profusion which characterises the Irish in everything, they had brought out large quantities of tobacco, whisky, and bunches of pipes. On such occasions it is the custom for those who attend the wake or the funeral to bring a full pipe home with them; and it is expected that as often as it is used they will remember to say, "God be merciful to the soul of him that this pipe was over."

The crowd, however, now began to disperse; and the immediate friends of the deceased sent the priest, accompanied by Kelly's brother, to request that we would come in, as the last mark of respect to poor Denis's memory, and take a glass of wine and a cake.

"Come, Toby," said my brother, "we may as well go in, as it will gratify them; we need not make much delay, and we will still be at home in sufficient time for dinner."

"Certainly you will," said the priest, "for you shall both come and dine with me to-day."

"With all my heart," said my brother—"I have no objection, for I know you give it good."

When we went in, the punch was already reeking from immense white jugs, that couldn't hold less than a gallon each.

"Now," said his reverence, very properly, "you have had a dacent and creditable funeral, and have managed everything with great propriety; let me request, therefore, that you will not get drunk, nor permit yourselves to enter into any disputes or quarrels, but be moderate in what you take, and go home peaceably."

"Why, thin, your reverence," replied the widow, "he's now in his grave, and, thank God, it's he that had the dacent funeral all out—ten good gallons did we put on you, *asthore*, and it's yourself that liked the dacent thing, anyhow; but sure, sir, it would shame him where he's lyin' if we disregarded him so far as to go home widout bringing in our friends that didn't desart us in our throuble, and thratin' them for their kindness."

While Kelly's brother was filling out all their glasses, the priest, my brother, and I were taking a little refreshment. When the glasses were filled, the deceased's brother raised his in his hand, and said—

73

"Well, gintlemen," addressing us, "I hope you'll pardon me for not dhrinking your healths first; but people, you know, can't break through an ould custom, at any rate—so I give poor Denis's health, that's in his warm grave, and God be marciful to his sowl." [1]

The priest now winked at me to give them their own way; so we filled our glasses, and joined with the rest in drinking "Poor Denis's health, that's now in his warm grave, and God be merciful to his soul."

When this was finished, they then drank ours, and thanked us for our kindness in attending the funeral. It was now past five o'clock, and we left them just setting in to a hard bout of drinking, and rode down to his reverence's residence.

"I saw you smile," said he, on our way, "at the blundering toast of Mat Kelly; but it would be labour in vain to attempt setting them right. What do they know about the distinctions of more refined life? Besides, I maintain that what they said was as well calculated to express their affection as if they had drunk honest Denis's memory. It is, at least, unsophisticated. But did you hear," said he, "of the apparition that was seen last night on the mountain road above Denis's?"

"I did not hear of it," I replied, equivocating a little.

"Why," said he, "it is currently reported that the spirit of a murdered pedlar, which haunts the hollow of the road at Drumfurrar, chased away the two servant-men as they were bringing home the coffin, and that finding it a good bit, he then got into it, and walked half a mile along the road with the wooden surtout upon him; and finally, that, to wind up the frolic, he left it on one end half-way between the bridge and Denis's house, after putting a crowd of the countrymen to flight. I suspect some droll knave has played them a trick. I assure you that a deputation of them, who declared that they saw the coffin move along of itself, waited upon me this morning to know whether they ought to have him put into the coffin or gotten another."

"Well," said my brother, in reply to him, "after dinner we will probably throw some light upon that circumstance; for I believe my brother here knows something about it."

[1] A fact.

74

"So, sir," said the priest, "I perceive you have been amusing yourself at their expense."

I seldom spent a pleasanter evening than I did with Father Molloy (so he was called), who was, as my brother said, a shrewd, sensible man, possessed of convivial powers of the first order. He sang us several good songs; and to do him justice, he had an excellent voice. He regretted very much the state of party and religious feeling, which he did everything in his power to suppress.

"But," said he, "I have little co-operation in my efforts to communicate knowledge to my flock and implant better feelings among them. You must know," he added, "that I am no great favourite among them. On being appointed to this parish by my bishop, I found that the young man who was curate to my predecessor had formed a party against me, thinking, by that means, eventually to get the parish himself. Accordingly, on coming here, I found the chapel doors closed on me; so that a single individual among them would not recognise me as their proper pastor. By firmness and spirit, however, I at length succeeded, after a long struggle against the influence of the curate, in gaining admission to the altar; and by a proper representation of his conduct to the bishop I soon made my gentleman knock under. Although beginning to gain ground in the good opinion of the people, I am by no means yet a favourite. The curate and I scarcely speak; and a great number of my parishioners brand me with the epithet of the "Orange priest," and this principally because I occasionally associate with Protestants—a habit, gentlemen, which they will find some difficulty in making me give up as long as I can have the pleasure," said he, bowing, "of seeing such guests at my table as those with whose company I am now honoured."

It was now near nine o'clock, and my brother was beginning to relate an anecdote concerning the clergyman who had preceded Father Molloy in the parish, when a messenger from Mr. Wilson, already alluded to, came up in breathless haste, requesting the priest for God's sake to go down into town instantly, as the Kellys and the Grimeses were engaged in a fresh quarrel.

"My God!" he exclaimed—"when will this work have an

end? But, to tell you the truth, gentlemen, I apprehended it; and I fear something still more fatal to the parties will yet be the consequence. Mr. D'Arcy, you must try what you can do with the Grimeses, and I will manage the Kellys."

We then proceeded to the town, which was but a very short distance from the priest's house; and on arriving, found a large crowd before the door of the house in which the Kellys had been drinking, engaged in hard conflict. The priest was on foot, and had brought his whip with him, it being an argument in the hands of a Roman Catholic pastor which tells so home that it is not to be gainsaid. Mr. Molloy and my brother now dashed in amongst them, and by remonstrance, abuse, blows, and entreaty, they with difficulty succeeded in terminating the fight. They were also assisted by Mr. Wilson and other persons, who dared not, until their appearance, run the risk of interfering between them. Wilson's servant who had come for the priest, was still standing beside me looking on; and while my brother and Mr. Molloy were separating the parties, I asked him how the fray commenced.

"Why, sir," said he, "it bein' market-day, the Grimeses chanced to be in town, and this got to the ears of the Kellys, who were drinking in Cassidy's here till they got tipsy; some then broke out, and began to go up and down the street, shouting for the face of a murdhering Grimes. The Grimeses, sir, happened at the time to be drinking with a parcel of their friends in Joe Sherlock's, and hearing the Kellys calling out for them, why, as the dhrop, sir, was in on both sides, they were soon at it. Grimes has given one of the Kellys a great bating; but Tom M'Guigan, Kelly's cousin, a little before we came, I'm tould, has knocked the seven senses out of him with the pelt of a brickbat in the stomach."

Soon after this, however, the quarrel was got under; and in order to prevent any more bloodshed that night, my brother and I got the Kellys together, and brought them as far as our residence on their way home. As we went along they uttered awful vows and determinations of the deepest revenge, swearing repeatedly that they would shoot Grimes from behind a ditch if they could not in any other manner have his blood. They seemed highly intoxicated, and several

76

of them were cut and abused in a dreadful manner; even the women were in such a state of excitement and alarm that grief for the deceased was in many instances forgotten. Several of both sexes were singing; some laughing with triumph at the punishment they had inflicted on the enemy; others of them, softened by what they had drunk, were weeping in tones of sorrow that might be heard a couple of miles off. Among the latter were many of the men, some of whom, as they staggered along, with their frieze big-coats hanging off one shoulder, clapped their hands and roared like bulls, as if they intended, by the loudness of their grief then, to compensate for their silence when sober. It was also quite ludicrous to see the men kissing each other, sometimes in this maudlin sorrow, and at others when exalted into the very madness of mirth. Such as had been cut in the scuffle, on finding the blood trickle down their faces, would wipe it off, then look at it, and break out into a parenthetical volley of curses against the Grimeses; after which they would resume their grief, hug each other in mutual sorrow, and clap their hands as before. In short, such a group could be seen nowhere but in Ireland.

When my brother and I had separated from them I asked him what had become of Vengeance, and if he were still in the country.

"No," said he; "with all his courage and watchfulness, he found that his life was not safe; he accordingly sold off his property, and collecting all his ready cash, emigrated to America, where, I hear, he is doing well."

"God knows," I replied, "I shouldn't be surprised if one half of the population were to follow his example, for the state of society here among the lower orders is truly deplorable."

"Ay, but you are to consider," said he, "that you have been looking at the worst of it. If you pass an unfavourable opinion upon our countrymen when in the public-house or the quarrel, you ought to remember what they are under their own roofs and in all the relations of public life."

THE MIDNIGHT MASS

FRANK M'KENNA was a snug farmer, frugal and industrious in his habits, and, what is rare amongst most men
of his class, addicted to neither drink nor quarrelling. He
lived at the skirt of a mountain, which ran up in long suc-
cessive undulations until it ended in a dark, abrupt peak, very
perpendicular on one side, and always, except on a bright
day, capped with clouds. Before his door lay a hard plain,
covered only with a kind of bent, and studded with round
grey rocks protruding somewhat above its surface. Through
this plain, over a craggy channel, ran a mountain torrent, that
issued, to the right of M'Kenna's house, from a rocky and
precipitous valley, which twisted itself round the base of the
mountain until it reached the perpendicular side, where the
peak actually overhung it. On looking either from the
bottom of the valley or the top of the peak, the depth
appeared immense ; and on a summer's day, when the black-
thorns and other hardy shrubs that in some places clothed its
rocky sides were green, to view the river sparkling below you
in the sun, as it flung itself over two or three cataracts of
great depth and boldness, filled the mind with those unde-
finable sensations of pleasure inseparable from a contemplation
of the sublimities of nature. Nor did it possess less interest
when beheld in the winter storm. Well do we remember,
though then ignorant of our own motives, when we have, in
the turmoil of the elements, climbed its steep, shaggy sides,
disappearing like a speck, or something not of earth, among
the dark clouds that rolled over its summit, for no other
purpose than to stand upon its brow and look down on the
red torrent dashing with impetuosity from crag to crag, whilst
the winds roared, and the clouds flew in dark columns around
us, giving to the natural wildness of the place an air of wilder
desolation. Beyond this glen the mountains stretched away
for eight or ten miles in swelling masses, between which lay

78

many extensive sweeps, well sheltered, and abundantly stocked with game, particularly with hares and grouse. M'Kenna's house stood, as I said, at the foot of this mountain, just where the yellow surface of the plain began to darken into the deeper hues of the heath; to the left lay a considerable tract of stony land in a state of cultivation; and beyond the river, exactly opposite the house, rose a long line of hills, studded with houses, and in summer diversified with fallow, pasture, and corn fields, the beauty of which was heightened by the columns of smoke that slanted across the hills as the breeze carried them through the lucid haze of the atmosphere.

M'Kenna's family consisted of himself, his wife, two daughters, and two sons. One of these was a young man addicted to drink, idle, ill-tempered, and disobedient; seldom taking a part in the labours of the family, but altogether devoted to field sports, fairs, markets, and dances. In many parts of Ireland it is usual to play at cards for mutton, loaves, fowls, or whisky, and he was seldom absent from such gambling parties if held within a reasonable distance. Often had the other members of the family remonstrated with him on his idle and immoral courses; but their remonstrances only excited his bad passions, and produced, on his part, angry and exasperating language, or open determinations to abandon the family altogether and enlist. For some years he went on in this way, a hardened, ungodly profligate, spurning the voice of reproof and of conscience, and insensible to the entreaties of domestic affection or the commands of parental authority. Such was his state of mind and mode of life when our story opens.

At the time in which the incidents contained in this sketch took place, the peasantry of Ireland, being less encumbered with heavy rents, and more buoyant in spirits than the decay of national prosperity has of late permitted them to be, indulged more frequently and to a greater stretch in those rural sports and festivities so suitable to their natural love of humour and amusement. Dances, wakes, and weddings were then held according to the most extravagant forms of ancient usage; the people were easier in their circumstances, and consequently indulged in them with lighter hearts and a stronger relish for enjoyment. When any of the great festivals of their religion approached, the popular mind, unrepressed by poverty and national dissension, gradually elevated itself to a species of wild and reckless mirth, productive of incidents irresistibly ludicrous and remarkably characteristic of Irish manners. It is not, however, to be expected that a people whose love of fighting is so innate a principle in their disposition should celebrate these festive seasons without an occasional crime, which threw its deep shadow over the mirthful character of their customs. Many such occurred; but they were looked upon then with a degree of horror and detestation of which we can form but a very inadequate idea at present.

It was upon the advent of one of those festivals—Christmas —that the family of M'Kenna, like every other family in the neighbourhood, were making preparations to celebrate it with the usual hilarity. They cleared out their barn in order to have a dance on Christmas Eve, and for this purpose the two sons and the servant man wrought with that kind of industry produced by the cheerful prospect of some happy event. For a week or fortnight before the evening on which the dance was appointed to be held, due notice of it had been given to the neighbours, and of course there was no doubt but that it would be numerously attended.

Christmas Eve, as the day preceding Christmas is called, has been always a day of great preparation and bustle. Indeed, the whole week previous to it is also remarkable, as exhibiting the importance attached by the people to those occasions on which they can give loose to their love of fun and frolic. The farmhouse undergoes a thorough cleansing. Father and sons are, or rather used to be, all engaged in repairing the outhouses, patching them with thatch where it was wanted, mending mangers, paving stable floors, fixing cow-stakes, making *boraghs*,[1] removing nuisances, and cleaning streets.

On the other hand, the mothers, daughters, and maids were also engaged in their several departments—the latter scouring the furniture with sand; the mother making culinary preparations, baking bread, killing fowls, or salting meat;

---

[1] The rope with which a cow is tied in the cow-house.

whilst the daughters were unusually intent upon the decoration of their own dress, and the making up of the family linen. All, however, was performed with an air of gaiety and pleasure; the ivy and holly were disposed about the dressers and collar beams with great glee; the chimneys were swept amidst songs and laughter; many bad voices, and some good ones, were put in requisition; whilst several who had never been known to chant a stave, alarmed the listeners by the grotesque and incomprehensible nature of their melody.. Those who were inclined to devotion—and there is no lack of it in Ireland—took to carols and hymns, which they sang, for want of better airs, to tunes highly comic. We have ourselves often heard the Doxology sung in Irish verse to the facetious air of "Paudeen O'Rafferty," and other hymns to the tune of "Peas upon a Trencher" and "Cruiskeen Lawn." Sometimes, on the contrary, many of them, from the very fulness of jollity, would become pathetic, and indulge in those touching old airs of their country which may be truly called songs of sorrow, from the exquisite and simple pathos with which they abound. This, though it may seem anomalous, is but natural; for there is nothing so apt to recall to the heart those friends, whether absent or dead, with whom it has been connected, as a stated festival. Affection is then awakened, and summons to the hearth where it presides those on whose faces it loves to look. If they be living, it places them in the circle of happiness which surrounds it; and if they be removed for ever from such scenes, their memory, which, amidst the din of ordinary life, has almost passed away, is now restored, and their loss felt as if it had been only just then sustained.

For this reason, at such times it is not at all unusual to see the elders of Irish families touched by pathos as well as humour. The Irish are a people whose affections are as strong as their imaginations are vivid; and, in illustration of this, we may add that many a time have we seen them raised to mirth and melted into tears, almost at the same time, by a song of the most comic character. The mirth, however, was for the song, and the sorrow for the memory of some beloved relation who had been remarkable for singing it or with whom it had been a favourite.

We do not affirm that in the family of the M'Kennas there were, upon the occasion which we are describing, any tears shed. The enjoyments of the season, and the humours of the expected dance, both combined to give them a more than usual degree of mirth and frolic. At an early hour all that was necessary for the due celebration of that night and the succeeding day had been arranged and completed. The whisky had been laid in, the Christmas candles bought, the barn cleared out, the seats laid—in short, everything in its place, and a place for everything. About one o'clock, however, the young members of the family began to betray some symptoms of uneasiness; nor was M'Kenna himself, though the *farithee*, or man of the house, altogether so exempt from what they felt as might, if the cause of it were known to our readers, be expected from a man of his years and experience.

From time to time one of the girls tripped out as far as the stile before the door, where she stood looking in a particular direction until her sight was fatigued.

"Och, och !" her mother exclaimed during her absence, "but that *colleen's* sick about Barny ; *musha*, but it would be the beautiful joke, all out, if he'd disappoint the whole of yees. Faix, it wouldn't be unlike the same man to go to wherever he can make most money—and, sure, small blame to him for that; what's one place to him more than another?"

"Hut !" M'Kenna replied, rising, however, to go out himself, "the *girsha's* makin' a *bauliore* of herself."

"An' where's yourself slippin' out to?" rejoined his wife, with a wink of shrewd humour at the rest. "I say, Frank, are you goin' to look for him too? *Mavrone*, but that's sinsible ! Why, thin, you snakin' ould rogue, is that the way wid you? Throth, I have often hard it said that 'one fool makes many;' but sure enough, 'an ould fool's worse nor any.' Come in here this minute, I say—walk back—you to have your horn up—faix, indeed !"

"Why, I am only goin' to get the small phaties boiled for the pigs, poor crathurs, for their Christmas dinner. Sure, we oughtn't to neglect thim no more than ourselves, the crathurs, that can't spake their wants except by gruntin'."

"Saints above !—the Lord forgive me for bringin' down their names upon a Christmas Eve !—but it's beside himself the man is—an' him knows that the phaties wor boiled an' made up in balls for them airly this mornin'!"

In the meantime the wife's good-natured attack upon her husband produced considerable mirth in the family. In consequence of what she said, he hesitated; but ultimately was proceeding towards the door, when the daughter returned, her brow flushed, and her eye sparkling with mirth and delight.

"Ha!" said the father, with a complacent smile, "all's right, Peggy; you seen him, *alanna*. The music's in your eye, *acushla*, an' the feet of you can't keep themselves off o' the ground; an' all bekase you seen Barny *Dhal* pokin' acrass the fields, wid his head up, an' his skirt stickin' out behind him wid *Granua Waile*."[1]

The father had conjectured properly, for the joy which animated the girl's countenance could not be misunderstood.

"Barny's comin'," she exclaimed, clapping her hands with great glee, "an' our Frank wid him; they're at the river, an' Frank has him on his back, and *Granua Waile* undher his arm! Come out, come out! You'll die for good, lookin' at them staggerin' acrass. I knew he'd come! I knew it! God be good to thim that invinted Christmas; it's a brave time, faix!"

In a moment the inmates were grouped before the door, all anxious to catch a glimpse of Barny and *Granua Waile*.

"Faix, ay!" "Sure enough!" "Sarra doubt of it!" "Whethen, I'd never mistrust Barny!" might be heard in distinct exclamations from each.

"Faith, he's a Trojan," said the *farithee*, "an' must get lashins of the best we have. Come in, childher, an' red the hob for him.

> 'Och, Christmas comes but wanst a year,
>   An' Christmas comes but wanst a year;
>   An' the divil a mouth
>   Shall be friends wid drouth,
>   While I have whisky, ale, or beer.

---

[1] Meaning his fiddle. It is one of the many names by which Ireland itself is designated in bardic erfusions, and is used in many of the country ballads of the present day. Granua Waile (or properly, Grainne Maol) was Grace O'Malley, a famous Irish chieftainess in Queen Elizabeth's time.—ED.

'Och, Christmas comes but wanst a year,
An' Christmas comes but wanst a year;
    Wid han' in han',
    An' can to can,
Then hi for the whisky, ale, an' beer.

'Och, Christmas comes but wanst a year,
An' Christmas comes but wanst a year;
    Then the high an' the low
    Shall shake their toe
When prim'd wid whisky, ale, an' beer.'

For all that, the sorra fig I care for either ale or beer, barrin'
in regard of mere drouth; give me the whisky. Eh, Alley,
won't we have a jorum, anyhow?"

"Why, thin," replied the wife, "the divil be from me (the
crass about us for namin' him), but you're a greater *Brine-oge*
than some of your childher! I suppose it's your capers
Frank has in him. Will you behave yourself, you ould sling-
poke? Behave, I say, an' let me go. Childher, will you
help me to flake this man out o' the place? Look at him
here, caperin' an' crackin' his fingers afore me, an' pullin' me
out to dance!"

"Och, och, murdher alive!" exclaimed the good man, out
of breath. "I seen the day, anyway—an' maybe could show
a step or two yet if I was well vexed. You can't forget
ould times, Alley? Eh, you thief?"

"*Musha*, have sinse, man alive," replied the wife, in a tone
of placid gravity, which only betrayed the pleasure she herself felt in his happiness. "Have sinse, an' the strange man
comin' in, an' don't let him see you in such figaries."

The observation of the good woman produced a loud laugh
among them. "*Arrah*, what are yees laughin' at?" she
inquired.

"Why, mother," said one of her daughters, "how could
Barny *Dhal*, a blind man, see anybody?"

Alley herself laughed at her blunder, but wittily replied,
"Faith, *avourneen*, maybe he can often see as nately through
his ear as you can do wid your eyes open; sure, they say he
can hear the grass growin'."

"For that matther," observed the *farithee*, joining in the
joke, "he can see as far as any of us—whin we're asleep."

84

The conversation was thus proceeding when Barny *Dahl* and young Frank M'Kenna entered the kitchen.

In a moment all hands were extended to welcome Barny: "*Millia failte ghud*, Barny!" "*Cead millia failte ghud*, Barny!" "Oh, Barny, did you come at last?" "You're welcome, Barny!" "Barny, my Trojan, how is every cart-load of you?" "How is *Granua Waile*, Barny?"

"Why, thin, holy music, did you never see Barny *Dhal* afore? Clear off from about me, or, by the sweets of rosin, I'll play the divil an' break things. 'You're welcome, Barny!' an' 'How are you, Barny?' Why, thin, piper o' Moses, don't I know I'm welcome, an' yit you must be tellin' me what everybody knows! But sure I have great news for you all!"

"What is that, Barny?"

"Well, but can yees keep a sacret?—can yees, girls?"

"Faix can we, Barny, *achora*."

"Well, so can I—ha, ha, ha! Now are yees sarved? Come, let me to the hob."

"Here, Barny; I'll lead you, Barny."

"No, I have him—come, Barny, I'll lead you; here, *achora*, this is the spot—that's it. Why, Barny," said the arch girl, as she placed him in the corner, "sorra one o' the hob but knows you; it never stirs—ha, ha, ha!"

"Throth, *a colleen*, that tongue o' yours will delude some one afore long, if it hasn't done so already."

"But how is *Granua Waile*, Barny?"

"Poor *Granua* is it? Faith, times is hard wid her often. '*Granua*,' says I to her, 'what do you say, *acushla*?—we're axed to go to two or three places to-day—what do you say? Do you lead, an' I'll follow; your will is my pleasure.' 'An' where are we axed to?' says *Granua*, sinsible enough. 'Why,' says I, 'to Paddy Lanigan's, to Mike Hartigan's, to Jack Lynch's, an', at the heel o' the hunt, to Frank M'Kenna's of the Mountain Bar.' 'By my song,' says she, 'you may go where you plase; for me, I'm off to Frank M'Kenna's, one of the dacentest men in Europe, an' his wife the same. Divil a toe I'll set a-waggin' in any other place this night,' says she, 'for 'tis there we're both well thrated wid the best the house can afford. So,' says she, 'in the

name of all that's musical, you're welcome to the poker an
tongs anywhere else; for me, I'm off to Frank's.' An' faith
sure enough, she took to her pumps; an' it was only comin'
over the hill there that young Frank an' I overtuck her—
divil a lie in it.''

In fact, Barny, besides being a fiddler, was a *shanahus* of
the first water; could tell a story or trace a genealogy as
well as any man living, and draw the long bow in either
capacity much better than he could in the practice of his
more legitimate profession.

"Well, here she is, Barny, to the fore,'' said the aforesaid
arch girl, " an' now give us a tune.''

"What!'' replied the *farithee*, " is it widout either aitin'
or dhrinkin'? Why, the *girsha's* beside herself! Alley, *aroon*,
get him the linin',[1] and a sup to tighten his elbow.''

The good woman instantly went to provide refreshments
for the musician.

"Come, girls,'' said Barny, "will yees get me a scythe or
a handsaw?''

" A scythe or a handsaw—ethen what to do, Barny?''

" Why, to pare my nail, to be sure,'' replied Barny, with a
loud laugh; "but stay—come back here—I'll make shift to
do wid a pair of scissors this bout.

> 'The paarent finds his sons,
> The tutherer whips them;
> The nailer makes his nails,
> The fiddler clips them.'"

Wherever Barny came there was mirth and a disposition
to be pleased, so that his jokes always told.

"*Musha*, the sorra pare you, Barny,'' said one of the girls,
"but there's no bein' up to you, good or bad.''

"The sorra pair me, is it? Faix, Nancy, you'll soon be
paired yourself wid some one, *avourneen*. Do you know a
sartin young man wid a nose on him runnin' to a point like
the pin of a sun-dial, his knees breakin' the king's pace, strikin'
one another ever since he was able to walk, an' that was
about four years afther he could say his *Pather Nosther*? an'

---

[1] That is, food and drink.

86

faith, whatever you may think, there's no makin' them pace-able except by puttin' between them! The wrong side of his shin, too, is foremost; an' though the one-half of his two feet is all heels, he keeps the same heels for set days an' bonfire nights, an' savinly walks on his ankles. His leg, too, Nancy, is stuck in the middle of his foot, like a poker in a pickaxe ; an', along wid all——"

"Here, Barny, thry your hand at this," said the good woman, who had not heard his ludicrous description of her fictitious son-in-law—"*eeh arran agus bee laudher,* Barny, ate bread an' be strong. I'll warrant when you begin to play they'll give you little time to do anything but scrape away. Taste the dhrink first, anyway, in the name o' God," and she filled him a glass.

"Augh, augh! faith, you're the moral [1] of a woman. Are you there, M'Kenna?—here's a sudden disholution to your family! May they be scattered wid all speed—manin' the girls—to all corners o' the parish!—ha, ha, ha! Well, that won't vex them, anyhow; an' next, here's a merry Chris'mas to us, an' many o' them! Whooh! blur-an-age! whooh! oh, by gorra!—that's—that's—Frank, run afther my breath—I've lost it—run, you tory [2]—oh, by gor, that's stuff as sthrong as Samson, so it is. Arrah, what well do you dhraw that from? for, faith, 'twould be mighty convanient to live near it in a hard frost."

Barny was now silent for some time, which silence was pro-duced by the industry he displayed in assailing the substantial refreshments before him. When he had concluded his repast he once more tasted the liquor, after which he got *Granua Waile,* and continued playing their favourite tunes, and amusing them with anecdotes, both true and false, until the hour drew nigh when his services were expected by the young men and maidens who had assembled to dance in the barn. Occasionally, however, they took a preliminary step, in which they were joined by a few of their neighbours. Old Frank himself felt his spirits elevated by contemplating the happiness of his children and their young associates.

[1] Model.
[2] It is curious that the words Whig and Tory have each an Irish origin. Tory is an Irish word meaning an outlaw or wanderer.—ED.

"Frank," said he, to the youngest of his sons, "go down to Owen Reillaghan's, and tell him an' his family to come up to the dance early in the evenin'. Owen's a pleasant man," he added, "and a good neighbour, but a small thought too strict in his duties. Tell him to come up, Frank, airly I say ; he'll have time enough to go to the Midnight Mass afther dancin' the 'Rakes of Ballyshanny' and the 'Baltihorum Jig' ; an' maybe he can't do both in style."

"Ay," said Frank, in his jeering manner, "he carries a handy heel at the dancin' and a supple tongue at the prayin' ; but let him alone for bringin' the bottom of his glass and his eyebrow acquainted. But if he'd pray less——"

"Go along, *a veehonee*, an' bring him up," replied the father—"you to talk about prayin' ! Them that ud catch you at a prayer ought to be showed for the world to wonder at : a man wid two heads an him would be a fool to him. Go along, I say, and do what you're bid."

"I'm goin'," said Frank, "I'm off ; but what if he doesn't come ? I'll then have my journey for nothin'."

"An' it's good payment for any journey ever you'll make, barrin' it's to the gallows," replied the father, provoked at his reluctance in obeying him. "Won't you have dancin' enough in the coorse o' the night, for you'll not go to the Midnight Mass, and why don't you be off wid you at wanst ?"

Frank shrugged his shoulders two or three times, being loth to leave the music and dancing ; but on seeing his father about to address him in sharper language, he went out with a frown on his brows and a half-smothered imprecation bursting from his lips.

He had not proceeded more than a few yards from the door when he met Rody Teague, his father's servant, on his way to the kitchen. "Rody," said he, "isn't this a purty business? my father wantin' to send me down to Owen Reillaghan's ; when, by the vartue o' my oath, I'd as soon go half-way into hell as to any place where his son, Mike Reillaghan, ud be. How will I manage, Rody ?"

"Why," replied Rody, "as to meetin' wid Mike, take my advice and avoid him. And what is more, I'd give up Peggy Gartland for good. Isn't it a mane thing for you, Frank, to

88

be hangin' afther a girl that's fonder of another than she is of yourself. By this and by that, I'd no more do it—*avouh!* catch me at it—I'd have spunk in me."

Frank's brow darkened as Rody spoke; instead of instantly replying, he was silent, and appeared to be debating some point in his own mind on which he had not come to a determination.

"My father didn't hear of the fight between Mike and me?" said he interrogatively — "do you think he did, Rody?"

"Not to my knowledge," replied the servant; "if he did, he wouldn't surely send you down. But talking of the fight, you are known to be a stout, well-fought boy—no doubt of that—still, I say, you'd no right to provoke Mike as you did, who, it's well known, could bate any two men in the parish; and so, sign's on it, you got yourself dacently trounced about a girl that doesn't love a bone in your skin."

"He disgraced me, Rody," observed Frank; "I can't rise my head; and you know I was thought by all the parish as good a man as him. No, I wouldn't this blessed Christmas Eve above us, for all that ever my name is worth, be disgraced by him as I am. But—hould, man—have patience!"

"Throth, and, Frank, that's what you never had," said Rody; "and as to bein' disgraced, you disgraced yourself. What right had you to challenge the boy to fight, and to strike him into the bargain, bekase Peggy Gartland danced wid him and wouldn't go out wid you? Death alive, sure that wasn't his fault."

Every word of reproof which proceeded from Rody's lips but strengthened Frank's rage and added to his sense of shame; he looked first in the direction of Reillaghan's house, and immediately towards the little village in which Peggy Gartland lived.

"Rody," said he, slapping him fiercely on the shoulder, "go in—I've—I've made up my mind upon what I'll do—go in, Rody, and get your dinner; but don't be out of the way when I come back."

"And what have you made up your mind to?" inquired Rody.

"Why, be the Sacred Mother o' Heaven, Rody, to—to— be friends wid Mike."

89

"Ay, there's sinse and rason in that," replied Rody; "and if you'd take my advice you'd give up Peggy Gartland too."

"I'll see you when I come back, Rody; don't be from about the place."

And as he spoke, a single spring brought him over the stile at which they held the foregoing conversation.

On advancing he found himself in one of his father's fields under the shelter of an elder hedge. Here he paused, and seemed still somewhat uncertain as to the direction in which he should proceed. At length he decided; the way towards Peggy Gartland's was that which he took, and as he walked rapidly he soon found himself at the village in which she lived.

It was now a little after twilight; the night was clear, the moon being in her first quarter, and the clouds through which she appeared to struggle were light and fleecy, but rather cold-looking—such, in short, as would seem to promise a sudden fall of snow. Frank had passed the first two cabins of the village, and was in the act of parrying the attacks of some yelping cur that assailed him, when he received a slap on the back, accompanied by a *gho manhi Dhea ghud, a Franchas, co wul thu guilh a nish, a rogora dhu?*

"Who's this?" exclaimed Frank—" eh! why, Darby More, you smilin' thief o' the world, is this you?"

"Ay, indeed; an' you're goin' down to Peggy's?" said the other, pointing significantly towards Peggy Gartland's house. "Well, man, what's the harm? She may get worse—that is, hopin' still that you'll mend your manners, *a bouchal*. But isn't your nose out o' joint there, Frank, darlin'?"

"No sich thing at all, Darby," replied Frank, gulping down his indignation, which rose afresh on hearing that the terms on which he stood with Peggy were so notorious.

"Throth but it is," said Darby; "an' to tell the blessed thruth, I'm not sarry that it's out o' joint; for when I tould you to lave the case in my hands, along wid a small thrifle o' silver that didn't signify much to you, whoo! not at all—you'd rather play it at cards, or dhrink it, or spind it wid no good. Out o' joint! *musha*, if ever a man's nose was to be pitied, yours is: why, didn't Mike Reillaghan put it out

90

o' joint twiist? first in regard to Peggy, and secondly by the batin' he gave you an it."

"It's well known, Darby," replied Frank, "that 'twas by a chance blow he did it; and you know a chance blow might kill the divil."

"But there was no danger of Mike's gettin' the chance blow," observed the sarcastic vagrant, for such he was.

"Maybe it's afore him," replied his companion; "we'll have another thrial for it, anyhow. But where are you goin,' Darby? Is it to the dance?"

"Me! Is it a man wid two holy ordhers an him? No, no! I might go up, maybe as far as your father's, merely to see the family, only for the night that's in it; but I'm goin' to another frind's place to spind my Chris'mas, an' over an' above I must go to the Midnight Mass. Frank, change your coorses an' mind your life, an' don't be the talk o' the parish. Remimber me to the family, an' say I'll see them soon."

"How long will you stop in the neighbourhood?" inquired Frank.

"*Arrah*, why, *acushla?*" replied the mendicant, softening his language.

"I might be wantin' to see you some o' these days," said the other—"indeed, it's not unlikely, Darby; so don't go, anyhow, widout seein' me."

"Ah!" said Darby, "had you taken a fool's advice—but it can't be helped—the harm's done, I doubt; how-an'-ever, for the matther o' that, maybe I have as good as Peggy in my eye for you. By the same token, as the night's cowld, warm your tooth, *avick;* there's waker wather nor this in Lough Corr. Sorra sup of it ever I keep for my own use at all, barrin' when I take a touch o' configuration in my bowels, or maybe when I'm too long at my prayers; for, God help me, sure I'm but sthrivin,' wid the help of one thing an' another, to work out my salvation as well as I can! Your health, anyhow, an' a merry Chris'mas to you!—not forgettin' myself," he added, putting to his lips a large cow's horn which he kept slung beneath his arm like the bugle of a coach-guard, only that this was generally concealed by an outside coat, no two inches of which were of the same material or colour. Having taken a tolerably large draught

91

from this, which, by the way, held near two quarts, he handed it, with a smack and a shrug, to Frank, who immediately gave it a wipe with the skirt of his coat, and pledged his companion.

"I'll be wantin'," observed Frank, "to see you in the hollydays—faith, that stuff's to be christened yet, Darby—so don't go till we have a dish o' discoorse about somethin' I'll mintion to you. As for Peggy Gartland, I'm done wid her; she may marry ould Nick for me."

"Or you for ould Nick," said the cynic, "which would be nearly the same thing. But go an, *avick*, an' never heed me; sure, I must have my spake—doesn't everybody know Darby More?"

"I've nothin' else to say now," added Frank, "and you have my authority to spread it as far as you plase. I'm done wid her; so good night, an' good cuttin' [1] to your horn, Darby!—You damn ould villain!" he subjoined, in a low voice, when Darby had got out of his hearing; "surely it's not in yourself, but in the blessed words and things you have about you, that there is any good."

"*Musha*, good night, Frank, *alanna*," replied the other; "an' the divil sweep you for a skamin' vagabone, that's a curse to the country, and has kep me out o' more weddins than any one I ever met wid, by your roguery in puttin' evil between frinds an' neighbours jist when they'd be ready for the priest to say the words over them. Good won't come of you, you profligate."

The last words were scarcely uttered by the sturdy mendicant, when he turned round to observe whether or not Frank would stop at Larry Gartland's, the father of the girl to whom he had hitherto unsuccessfully avowed his attachment.

"I'd depind on him," said he, in a soliloquy, "as soon as I'd depind upon ice of an hour's growth; an' whether or not, sure as I'm an my way to Owen Reillaghan's, the father of the dacent boy that he's strivin' to outdo, mayn't I as well watch his motions, anyway?"

He accordingly proceeded along the shadowy side of the street, in order to avoid Frank's eye, should he chance to

[1] Good cuttin'—May what's in it never fail.

92

look back, and quietly dodged on until he fairly saw him enter the house.

Having satisfied himself that the object of Frank's visit to the village was in some shape connected with Peggy Gartland, the mendicant immediately retraced his steps, and, at a pace more rapid than usual, strided on to Owen Reillaghan's, whither he arrived just in time to secure an excellent Christmas Eve dinner.

In Ireland that description of mendicants which differs so strikingly from the common crowd of beggars as to constitute a distinct species, comprehends within itself as anomalous an admixture of fun and devotion, external rigour and private licentiousness, love of superstition and of good whisky, as might naturally be supposed, without any great stretch of credulity, to belong to men thrown among a people in whom so many extremes of character and morals meet. The known beggar, who goes his own rounds, and has his own walk, always adapts his character to that of his benefactor, whose whims and peculiarities of temper he studies with industry, and generally with success. By this means, joined to a dexterity in tracing out the private history of families and individuals, he is enabled to humour the caprices, to manage the eccentricities, and to touch with a masterly hand the prejudices and particular opinions of his patrons; and this he contrives to do with great address and tact. Such was the character of Darby More, whose person, naturally large, was increased to an enormous size by the number of coats, blankets, and bags with which he was encumbered. A large belt buckled round his body, contained within its girth much more of money, meal, and whisky than ever met the eye; his hat was exceedingly low in the crown; his legs were cased in at least three pairs of stockings; and in his hand he carried a long cant, spiked at the lower end, with which he slung himself over small rivers and dykes, and kept dogs at bay. He was a devotee, too, notwithstanding the whisky-horn under his arm; attending wakes, christenings, and weddings; rubbed for the rose [1] and king's evil (for the varlet insisted that he was a seventh son); cured toothaches, colics, and

---

[1] A scrofulous swelling.

headaches by charms; but made most money by a knack which he possessed of tattooing into the naked breast the representation of Christ upon the cross. This was a secret of considerable value, for many of the superstitious people believed that by having this stained in upon them they would escape unnatural deaths, and be almost sure of heaven.

When Darby approached Reillaghan's house he was considering the propriety of disclosing to his son the fact of his having left his rival with Peggy Gartland. He ultimately determined that it would be proper to do so; for he was shrewd enough to suspect that the wish Frank had expressed of seeing him before he left the country was but a *ruse* to purchase his silence touching his appearance in the village. In this, however, he was mistaken.

"God save the house!" exclaimed Darby, on entering— "God save the house, an' all that's in it! God save it to the north!" and he formed the sign of the cross in every direction to which he turned; "God save it to the south! ✠ to the aiste! ✠ and to the wist! ✠ Save it upwards! ✠ and save it downwards! ✠ Save it backwards! ✠ and save it forwards! ✠ Save it right! ✠ and save it left! ✠ Save it by night! ✠ save it by day! ✠ Save it here! ✠ save it there! ✠ Save it this way! ✠ an' save it that way! ✠ Save it atin'! ✠ ✠ ✠ an' save it drinkin'! ✠ ✠ ✠ ✠ ✠ ✠ ✠ ✠ Oxis Doxis Glorioxis—Amin. An' now that I've blessed the place in the name of the nine Patriarchs, how are yees all, man, woman, and child? An' a merry Christmas to yees, says Darby More."

Darby, in the usual spirit of Irish hospitality, received a sincere welcome, was placed up near the fire, a plate filled with the best food on the table laid before him, and requested to want nothing for the asking.

"Why, Darby," said Reillaghan, "we expected you long ago; why didn't you come sooner?"

"The Lord's will be done! for ev'ry man has his throubles," replied Darby, stuffing himself in the corner like an epicure; "an' why should a sinner like me, or the likes o' me, be widout thim? 'Twas a dhrame I had last night that kep me. They say, indeed, that dhrames go by contraries, but not always, to my own knowledge."

"And what was the dhrame about, Darby?" inquired Reillaghan's wife.

"Why, ma'am, about some that I see on this hearth, well an' in good health. May they long live to be so! Oxis Doxis Glorioxis—Amin!" ✠ ✠ ✠

"Blessed Virgin! Darby, sure it would be nothin' bad that's to happen—would it, Darby?"

"Keep yourself asy on that head. I have widin my own mind the power of makin' it come out for good—I know the prayer for it. Oxis Doxis!" ✠ ✠

"God be praised for that, Darby; sure it would be a terrible business, all out, if anything was to happen. Here's Mike, that was born on Whissle Monday,[1] of all days in the year, an,' you know, they say that any child born on that day is to die an unnatural death. We named Mike after St. Michael, that he might purtect him."

"Make yourself asy, I say; don't I tell you I have the prayer to keep it back—hach! hach!—why, there's a bit stuck in my throath, some way! *Wurrah dheelish,* what's this! Maybe you could give me a sup o' dhrink—wather, or anything—to moisten the morsel I'm 'atin'? *Wurrah,* ma'am dear, make haste, it's goin' agin the breath wid me!"

"Oh, the sorra taste o' wather, Darby," said Owen; "sure this is Christmas Eve, you know; so you see, Darby, for ould acquaintance' sake, an' that you may put up an odd prayer now an' thin for us, jist be thryin' this."

Darby honoured the gift by immediate acceptance.

"Well, Owen Reillaghan," said he, "you make me take more o' this stuff nor any man I know; and particularly by rason that bein' given, wid a blessin', to the *ranns,* an' prayers, an' holy charms, I don't think it so good; barrin', indeed, as Father Dannellan tould me, when the wind, by long fastin', gets into my stomach, as was the case to-day, I'm often throubled, God help me, wid a configuration in the—hugh! ugh!—and thin it's good for me—a little of it."

"This would make a brave powdher-horn, Darby More,"

---

[1] Any child born on Whit Sunday or the day after is believed by the more ignorant to be doomed to an unnatural death.

observed one of Reillaghan's sons, "if it wasn't so big. What do you keep in it, Darby?"

"Why *a villish*, nothin', indeed, but a sup o' Father Dannellan's holy wather, that they say, by all accounts, it cost him great trouble to make, by rason that he must fast a long time, and pray by the day, afore he gets himself holy enough to consecrate it."

"It smells like whisky, Darby," said the boy, without any intention, however, of offending him; "it smells very like *poteen*."

"Hould yer tongue, Risthard," said the elder Reillaghan; "what ud make the honest man have whisky in it? Didn't he tell you what's in it?"

"The *gorsoon's* right enough," replied Darby; "I got the horn from Barny Dalton a couple o' days agone; 'twas whisky he had in it, an' it smells of it sure enough, an' will indeed for some time longer. Och! och! the heavens be praised, I've made a good dinner! May they never know want that gave it to me! Oxis Doxis Glorioxis—Amin!" ✠ ✠ ✠

"Darby, thry this agin," said Reillaghan, offering him another bumper.

"Throth an' I will, thin, for I find myself a great dale the betther of the one I tuck. Well, here's health an' happiness to us, an' may we all meet in heaven! Risthard, hand me that horn till I be going out to the barn, in ordher to do somethin' for my sowl. The holy wather's a good thing to have about one."

"But the dhrame, Darby?" inquired Mrs. Reillaghan. "Won't you tell it to us?"

"Let Mike follow me to the barn," he replied, "an' I'll tell him as much of it as he ought to hear. An' now let all of yees prepare for the Midnight Mass: go there wid proper intintions, an' not to be coortin' or dhrinking by the way. We're all sinners, anyway, an' oughtn't to neglect our sowls. Oxis Doxis Glorioxis. Amin!"

He immediately strode, with the horn under his arm, towards the barn, where he knelt, and began his orisons in a tone sufficiently loud to be heard in the kitchen.

When he was gone, Mrs. Reillaghan, who, with the curiosity natural to her sex, and the superstition peculiar to her station

96

in life, felt anxious to hear Darby's dream, urged Mike to follow him forthwith, that he might prevail on him to detail it at full length.

Darby, who knew not exactly what the dream ought to be, replied to Mike's inquiries vaguely.

"Mike," said he, "until the proper time comes, I can't tell it; but listen, take my advice an' slip down to Peggy Gartland's by-and-by. I have strong suspicions, if my dhrame is thrue, that Frank M'Kenna has a design upon her. People may be abroad this night widout bein' noticed by rason o' the Midnight Mass; Frank has friends in Kilnaheery, up behind the mountains, an' the divil might timpt him to bring her there. Keep your eye an him, or rather an Peggy. If my dhrame's true, he was there this night."

"I thought I gave him enough on her account," said Mike. "The poor girl hasn't a day's pace in regard of him; but, plase goodness, I'll soon put an end to it, for I'll marry her durin' the hollydays."

"Go, *avick*, an' let me finish my *Padareen Partha;* I have to get through it before the Midnight Mass comes. Slip down and find out what he was doin', and when you come back let me know."

Mike, perfectly aware of young M'Kenna's character, immediately went towards Lisdrum, for so the village where Peggy Gartland lived was called. He felt the danger to be apprehended from the interference of his rival the more acutely, inasmuch as he was not ignorant of the feuds and quarrels which the former had frequently produced between friends and neighbours by the subtle poison of his falsehoods, which were both wanton and malicious. He therefore advanced at an unusually brisk pace, and had nearly reached the village when he perceived in the distance a person resembling Frank approaching him at a pace nearly as rapid as his own.

"If it's Frank M'Kenna," thought he, "he must pass me, for this is his straight line home."

It appeared, however, that he had been mistaken; for he whom he had supposed to be the object of his enmity crossed the field by a different path, and seemed to be utterly ignorant of the person whom he was about to meet, so far at least as a quick, free, unembarrassed step could intimate his unacquaintance with him.

The fact, however, was that Reillaghan, had the person whom he met approached him more nearly, would have found his first suspicions correct. Frank was then on his return from Gartland's, and no sooner perceived Reillaghan, whom he immediately recognised by his great height, than he took another path in order to avoid him. The enmity between these rivals was deep and implacable; aggravated on the one hand by a sense of unmerited injury, and on the other by personal defeat and the bitterest jealousy. For this reason neither of them wished to meet, particularly Frank M'Kenna, who not only hated but feared his enemy.

Having succeeded in avoiding Reillaghan, the latter soon reached home; but here he found the door closed, and the family, with a single exception, in the barn, which was now nearly crowded with the youngsters of both sexes from the surrounding villages.

Frank's arrival among them gave a fresh impulse to their mirth and enjoyment. His manners were highly agreeable, and his spirits buoyant almost to levity. Notwithstanding the badness of his character in the opinion of the sober, steady, and respectable inhabitants of the parish, yet he was a favourite with the dissolute and thoughtless, and with many who had not an opportunity of seeing him except in his most favourable aspect. Whether he entertained on this occasion any latent design that might have induced him to assume a frankness of manner and an appearance of good humour which he did not feel, it is difficult to determine. Be this as it may, he made himself generally agreeable, saw that every one was comfortable, suggested an improvement in the arrangement of the seats, broke several jests on Barny and *Granua Waile*—which, however, were returned with interest—and in fact acquitted himself so creditably that his father whispered with a sigh to his mother—

"Alley, *achora*, wouldn't we be the happy family if that misfortunate boy of ours was to be always the thing he appears to be? God help him! the *gommach*, if he had sinse and the fear o' God before him, he'd not be sich a piece o' desate to sthrangers, and sich a divil's limb wid ourselves;

but he's young, an' may see his evil coorses in time wid the help o' God."

"*Musha*, may God grant it!" exclaimed his mother. "A fine slip he is, if his heart ud only turn to the right thoughts. One can't help feelin' pride out o' him when they see him actin' wid any kind o' rason."

The Irish dance, like every other assembly composed of Irishmen and Irishwomen, presents the spectator with those traits which enter into our conception of rollicking fun and broad humour. The very arrangements are laughable; and when joined to the eccentric strains of some blind fiddler like Barny *Dhal*, to the grotesque and caricaturish faces of the men, and the modest but evidently arch and laughter-loving countenances of the females, they cannot fail to impress an observing mind with the obvious truth that a nation of people so thoughtless and easily directed from the serious and useful pursuits of life to such scenes can seldom be industrious and wealthy, nor, despite their mirth and humour, a happy people.

The barn in which they danced on this occasion was a large one. Around the walls were placed as many seats as could be spared from the neighbours' houses; these were eked out by sacks of corn laid lengthwise, logs of round timber, old creels, iron pots with their bottoms turned up, and some of them in their usual position. On these were the youngsters seated; many of the "boys" with their sweethearts on their knees, the arms of the fair ones lovingly around their necks; and, on the contrary, many of the young women with their bachelors on their laps, their own necks also gallantly encircled by the arms of their admirers. Up in a corner sat Barny, surrounded by the seniors of the village, sawing the fiddle with indefatigable vigour, and leading the conversation with equal spirit. Indeed, his laugh was the loudest and his joke the best, whilst ever and anon his music became perfectly furious—that is to say, when he rasped the fiddle with a desperate effort "to overtake the dancers," from whom, in the heat of the conversation, he had unwittingly lagged behind.

Dancing in Ireland, like everything else connected with the amusement of the people, is frequently productive of bloodshed. It is not unusual for crack dancers from opposite parishes or from distant parts of the same parish to meet and dance against each other for victory; but as the judges in those cases consist of the respective friends or factions of the champions, their mode of decision may readily be conjectured. Many a battle is fought in consequence of such challenges, the result usually being that not he who has the lightest heel, but the hardest head, generally comes off the conqueror.

While the usual variety of Irish dances—the reel, jig, fling, three-part-reel, four-part-reel, rowly-powly, country-dance, *cotillon* (or cut-along, as the peasantry call it), and minuet, (vulgarly, minion, and minionet)—were going forward in due rotation, our readers may be assured that those who were seated around the walls did not permit the time to pass without improving it. Many an attachment is formed at such amusements, and many a bitter jealousy is excited; the prude and coquette, the fop and rustic Lothario, stand out here as prominently to the eye of him who is acquainted with human nature as they do in similar assemblies among the great; perhaps more so, as there is less art, and a more limited knowledge of intrigue to conceal their natural character.

The dance in Ireland usually commences with those who sit next the door, from whence it goes round with the sun. In this manner it circulates two or three times, after which the order is generally departed from, and they dance according as they can. This neglect of the established rule is also a fertile source of discord; for when two persons rise at the same time, if there be not room for both, the right of dancing first is often decided by blows.

At the dance we are describing, however, there was no dissension: every heart appeared to be not only elated with mirth, but also free from resentment and jealousy. The din produced by the thumping of vigorous feet upon the floor, the noise of the fiddle, the chat between Barny and the little sober knot about him, together with the brisk murmur of the general conversation, and the expression of delight which sat on every countenance, had something in them elevating to the spirits.

Barny, who knew the voices, and even the mode of dancing peculiar to almost every one in the barn, had some joke for each. When a young man brings out his sweetheart—which he frequently does in a manner irresistibly ludicrous, sometimes giving a spring from the earth, his *caubeen* set with a knowing air on one side of his head, advancing at a trot on tiptoe, catching her by the ear, leading her out to her position, which is "to face the fiddler," then ending by a snap of the fingers and another spring, in which he brings his heel backwards in contact with his ham—we say, when a young man brings out his sweetheart, and places her facing the fiddler, he asks her what she will dance ; to which, if she has no favourite tune, she uniformly replies, "Your will is my pleasure." This usually made Barny groan aloud.

"What ails you, Barny ?"

"Oh, thin, murdher alive, how little thruth's in this world ! 'Your will's my pleasure !' *Baithershin !* but, sowl, if things goes an, it won't be long so !"

"Why, Barny," the young man would exclaim, "is the ravin' fit comin' over you ?"

"No, in throth, Jim ; but it's thinkin' of home I am. How-and-iver, do you go an; but *naboclish !* what'll you have ?"

"'Jig Polthogue,' Barny ; but oil your wrist, *a bouchal,* or Katty will lave us both out o' sight in no time. Whoo ! success ! clear the coorse ! Well done, Barny ! That's the go !"

When the youngsters had danced for some time, the fathers and mothers of the village were called upon "to step out." This was generally the most amusing scene in the dance. No excuse is ever taken on such occasions; for, when they refuse, about a dozen young fellows place them, will they, nil they, upright upon the floor, from whence neither themselves nor their wives are permitted to move until they dance. No sooner do they commence than they are mischievously pitted against each other by two sham parties, one encouraging the wife, the other cheering on the good man ; whilst the fiddler, falling in with the frolic, plays in his most furious style. The simplicity of character, and perhaps the lurking vanity of those who are the butts of the mirth on this occasion, frequently heighten the jest.

"Why, thin, Paddy, is it strivin' to outdo me you are ? Faiks, *avourneen,* you never seen that day, anyway," the old woman would exclaim, exerting all her vigour.

"Didn't I! Sowl, I'll sober you before I lave the flure, for all that," her husband would reply.

"An' do you forget," she would rejoin, "that the M'Carthy dhrop is in me; ay, an' it's to the good still."

And the old dame would accompany the boast with a fresh attempt at agility; to which Paddy would respond by "cutting the buckle" and snapping his fingers; whilst fifty voices, amidst roars of laughter, were loud in encouraging each.

"Handle your feet, Katty darlin'—the mettle's lavin' him!"

"Off wid the brogues, Paddy, or she'll do you. That's it—kick off the other, an' don't spare the flure."

"A thousand guineas an Katty! M'Carthy agin Gallagher for ever!—whirroo!"

"Blur alive, the flure's not benefitin' by you, Paddy. Lay an it, man!—that's it!—bravo!—whish!—our side agin Europe!"

"Success, Paddy! Why, you could dance the 'Dusty Miller' upon a flure paved wid drawn razures, you're so soople."

"Katty for ever! The blood's in you, Katty; you'll win the day, *a ban choir!* More power to you!"

"I'll hould a quart on Paddy. Heel an' toe, Paddy, you sinner!"

"Right an' left, Katty—hould an, his breath's goin'."

"Right an' wrong, Paddy, you *spalpeen.* The whisky's an you, man alive; do it dacently, an' don't let me lose the wager."

In this manner would they incite some old man, and perhaps his older wife, to prolonged exertion, and keep them bobbing and jigging about amidst roars of laughter, until the worthy couple could dance no longer.

During stated periods of the night those who took the most prominent part in the dance got a plate and hat, with which they went round the youngsters, to make collections for the fiddler. Barny reserved his best and most sarcastic jokes for these occasions; for so correct was his ear that he felt little difficulty in detecting those whose contributions to him were such as he did not relish.

The aptitude of the Irish for enjoying humorous images

102

was well displayed by one or two circumstances which occurred on this night. A few of both sexes, who had come rather late, could get no other seats than the iron pots to which we have alluded. The young women were dressed in white, and their companions, who were also their admirers, exhibited, in proud display, each a brand new suit, consisting of broadcloth coat, yellow buff vests, and corduroy small-clothes, with a bunch of broad silk ribbons standing out at each knee. They were the sons and daughters of respectable farmers; but as all distinctions here entirely ceased, they were fain to rest contented with such seats as they could get, which on this occasion consisted of the pots aforesaid. No sooner, however, had they risen to dance than the house was convulsed with laughter, heightened by the sturdy vigour with which, unconscious of their appearance, they continued to dance. That part of the white female dresses which had come in contact with the pots exhibited a circle like the full moon, and was black as pitch. Nor were their partners more lucky; those who sat on the mouths of the pots had the back part of their dresses streaked with dark circles, equally ludicrous. The mad mirth with which they danced, in spite of their grotesque appearance, was irresistible. This, and other incidents quite as pleasant—such as the case of a wag who purposely sank himself into one of the pots, until it stuck to him through half the dance—increased the laughter, and disposed them to peace and cordiality.

No man took a more active part in these frolics than young Frank M'Kenna. It is true a keen eye might have noticed under his gaiety something of a moody and dissatisfied air. As he moved about from time to time, he whispered something to above a dozen persons who were well known in the country as his intimate companions, young fellows whose disposition and character were notoriously bad. When he communicated the whisper, a nod of assent was given by his confidants, after which it might be remarked that they moved round to the door with a caution that betrayed a fear of observation, and quietly slunk out of the barn, though Frank himself did not immediately follow them. In about a quarter of an hour afterwards Rody came in, gave him a signal, and sat down. Frank then followed his companions, and after a few minutes Rody also disappeared. This was about ten o'clock, and the dance was proceeding with great gaiety and animation.

Frank's dread of openly offending his parents prevented him from assembling his associates in the dwelling-house; the only convenient place of rendezvous, therefore, of which they could avail themselves was the stable. Here they met, and Frank, after uncorking a bottle of poteen, addressed them to the following effect:—

"Boys, there's great excuse for me in regard of my fight wid Mike Reillaghan; that you'll all allow. Come, boys, your healths! I can tell yees you'll find this good, the divil a doubt of it—be the same token, that I stole it from my father's Christmas drink; but no matther for that—I hope we'll never do worse. So, as I was sayin', you must bear me out as well as you can when I'm brought before the Diligates to-morrow for challengin' and strikin' a brother.[1] But I think you'll stand by me, boys?"

"By the tarn-o'-war, Frank, myself will fight to the knees for you."

"Faith, you may depend on us, Frank, or we're not to the fore."

"I know it, boys; and now for a piece of fun for this night. You see—come, Lanty, tare-an-ounkers, drink, man alive—you see, wid regard to Peggy Gartland—eh? what the hell! is that a cough?"

"One o' the horses, man—go an."

"Rody, did Darby More go into the barn before you came out of it?"

"Darby More?—not he. If he did, I'd a seen him, surely."

"Why, thin, I'd kiss the book I seen him goin' towards the barn as I was comin' into the stable. Sowl, he's a made boy, that; an' if I don't mistake, he's in Mike Reillaghan's intherest. You know devil a sacret can escape him."

"Hut! the prayin' ould crathur was on his way to the Midnight Mass; he thravels slow, and, of coorse, has to set

<hr>

[1] Those connected with illegal combinations are sworn to have no private or personal quarrels, not to strike, nor provoke each other to fight. Frank and Mike were members of such societies.

out early; besides, you know, he has carols, and bades, and the likes, to sell at the chapel."

"Thrue for you, Rody; why, I thought he might take it into his head to watch my motions, in regard that, as I said, I think him in Mike's intherest."

"Nonsense, man, what the dickens ud bring him into the stable loft? Why, you're beside yourself!"

"Begor, I bleeve so, but no matther. Boys, I want yees to stand to me to-night. I'm given to know for a sartinty that Mike and Peggy will be buckled to durin' the hollydays. Now I wish to get the girl myself; for if I don't get her, may I be ground to atoms if he will."

"Well, but how will you manage? for she's fond of him."

"Why, I'll tell you that. I was over there this evenin', and I understand that all the family is goin' to the Midnight Mass, barrin' herself. You see, while they're all gone to the 'mallet-office,'¹ we'll slip down wid a thrifle o' soot on our mugs, and walk off wid her to Kilnaheery, beyant the mountains, to an uncle's o' mine; an' after that let any man marry her who chooses to run the risk. Be the contints o' the book, Atty, if you don't dhrink I'll knock your head agin the wall, you *gommach!*"

"Why, thin, by all that's beautiful, it's a good spree; an' we'll stick to you like pitch."

"Be the vartue o' my oath, you don't desarve to be in it, or you'd dhrink dacent. Why, here's another bottle, an' maybe there's more where that was. Well, let us finish what we have, or, be the five crasses, I'll give up the whole business."

"Why, thin, here's success to us, anyway; an' high hangin' to them that ud desart you in your skame this blessed an' holy night that's in it!"

This was re-echoed by his friends, who pledged themselves by the most solemn oaths not to abandon him in the perpetration of the outrage which they had concerted. The other bottle was immediately opened, and while it lasted the details of the plan were explained at full length. This over, they entered the barn one by one, except Frank and Rody, who,

¹ Attending mass is called "going to the mallet-office"—an allusion to the beating of breasts in prayers.—ED.

105

as they were determined to steal another bottle from the father's stock, did not appear among the dancers until this was accomplished.

The reappearance of these rollicking and reckless young fellows in the dance was hailed by all present; for their outrageous mirth was in character with the genius of the place. The dance went on with spirit; brag dancers were called upon to exhibit in hornpipes, and for this purpose a table was brought in from Frank's kitchen, on which they performed in succession, each dancer applauded by his respective party as the best in the barn.

In the meantime the night had advanced; the hour might be about half-past ten o'clock; all were in the zenith of enjoyment, when old Frank M'Kenna addressed them as follows:—

"Neighbours, the dickens o' one o' me would like to break up the sport—an', in troth, harmless and dacent sport it is; but you all know that this is Christmas night, and that it's our duty to attind the Midnight Mass. Anybody that likes to hear it may go, for it's near time to be home an' prepare for it; but the sorra one o' me wants to take any of yees from your sport, if you prefer it—all I say is that I must lave yees; so God be wid yees till we meet agin!"

This short speech produced a general bustle in the barn; many of the elderly neighbours left it, and several of the young persons also. It was Christmas Eve, and the Midnight Mass had from time immemorial so strong a hold upon their prejudices and affections that the temptation must indeed have been great which would have prevented them from attending it. When old Frank went out, about one-third of those who were present left the dance along with him, and, as the hour for mass was approaching, they lost no time in preparing for it.

The Midnight Mass is, no doubt, a phrase familiar to our Irish readers; but we doubt whether those in the sister kingdoms who may honour our book with a perusal would, without a more particular description, clearly understand it.

This ceremony was performed as a commemoration not only of the night but of the hour in which Christ was born. To connect it either with edification or the abuse of religion would be invidious; so we overlook that, and describe it as it existed within our own memory, remarking by the way, that though now generally discontinued, it is in some parts of Ireland still observed, or has been till within a few years ago.

The parish in which the scene of this story is laid was large, consequently the attendance of the people was proportionably great. On Christmas Day a Roman Catholic priest has, or is said to have, the privilege of saying three masses, though on every other day in the year he can celebrate but two. Each priest, then, said one at midnight, and two on the following day.

Accordingly, about twenty or thirty years ago the performance of the Midnight Mass was looked upon as an ordinance highly important and interesting. The preparations for it were general and fervent; so much so, that not a Roman Catholic family slept till they heard it. It is true it only occurred once a year; but had any person who saw it once been called upon to describe it, he would say that religion could scarcely present a scene so wild and striking.

The night in question was very dark, for the moon had long disappeared, and as the inhabitants of the whole parish were to meet in one spot, it may be supposed that the difficulty was very great of traversing, in the darkness of midnight, the space between their respective residences and the place appointed by the priest for the celebration of mass. This difficulty they contrived to surmount. From about eleven at night till twelve or one o'clock the parish presented a scene singularly picturesque, and, to a person unacquainted with its causes, altogether mysterious. Over the surface of the surrounding country were scattered myriads of blazing torches, all converging to one point; whilst at a distance, in the central part of the parish, which lay in a valley, might be seen a broad focus of red light, quite stationary, with which one or more of the torches that moved across the fields mingled every moment. These torches were of bog-fir, dried and split for the occasion. All persons were accordingly furnished with them, and by their blaze contrived to make way across the country with comparative ease. This mass, having been especially associated with festivity and enjoyment, was always attended by such excessive numbers that the ceremony was in most parishes celebrated in the open air, if the weather were at all favourable. ; Altogether, as we have said, the appearance of the country at this dead hour of the night was wild and impressive. Being Christmas, every heart was up, and every pocket replenished with money, if it could at all be procured. This general elevation of spirits was nowhere more remarkable than in contemplating the thousands of both sexes, old and young, each furnished, as before said, with a blazing flambeau of bog-fir, all streaming down the mountain-sides, along the roads, or across the fields, and settling at last into one broad sheet of fire. Many a loud laugh might then be heard ring-- ing the night echo into reverberation; mirthful was the gabble in hard, guttural Irish; and now and then a song from some one whose potations had been rather copious would rise on the night breeze, to which a chorus was sub-joined by a dozen voices from the neighbouring groups.

On passing the *shebeen* and public-houses, the din of mingled voices that issued from them was highly amusing, made up, as it was, of songs, loud talk, rioting, and laughter, with an occasional sound of weeping from some one who had become penitent in his drink. In the larger public-houses (for in Ireland there usually are one or two of these in the immediate vicinity of each chapel) family parties were assembled, who set in to carouse both before and after mass. Those, how-ever, who had any love affairs on hand generally selected the shebeen house, as being private, and less calculated to expose them to general observation. As a matter of course, these jovial orgies frequently produced such disastrous consequences both to human life and female reputation, that the intrigues between the sexes, the quarrels, and violent deaths resulting from them ultimately occasioned the discontinuance of a ceremony which was only productive of evil. To this day it is an opinion among the peasantry in many parts of Ireland that there is something unfortunate connected with all drinking bouts held upon Christmas Eve. Such a prejudice naturally arises from a recollection of the calamities which so frequently befell many individuals while Midnight Masses were in the habit of being celebrated.

None of Frank M'Kenna's family attended mass but himself and his wife. His children, having been bound by all the rules of courtesy to do the honours of the dance, could not absent themselves from it; nor indeed were they disposed to do so. Frank, however, and his "good woman" carried their torches, and joined the crowds which flocked to this scene of fun and devotion.

When they had arrived at the cross-roads beside which the chapel was situated, the first object that presented itself so prominently as to attract observation was Darby More, dressed out in all his paraphernalia of blanket and horn, in addition to which he held in his hand an immense torch, formed into the figure of a cross. He was seated upon a stone, surrounded by a ring of old men and women, to whom he sang and sold a variety of Christmas carols, many of them rare curiosities in their way, inasmuch as they were his own composition. A little beyond them stood Mike Reillaghan and Peggy Gartland, towards both of whom he cast from time to time a glance of latent humour and triumph. He did not simply confine himself to singing his carols, but during the pauses of the melody addressed the wondering and attentive crowd as follows :—

"Good Christians—this is the day—how-and-iver, it's night now, glory be to God—that the angel Lucifer appeared to Shud'orth,[1] Meeshach, an' To-bed-we-go, in the village of Constantinople, near Jerooslem. The heavens be praised for it, 'twas a blessed an' holy night, an' remains so from that day to this—Oxis Doxis Glorioxis, Amin! Well, the sarra one of him but appeared to thim at the hour o' midnight; but they were asleep at the time, you see, and didn't persave him; so wid that he pulled out a horn like mine—an', by the same token, it's lucky to wear horns about one from that day to this—an' he put it to his lips an' tuck a good dacent—I mane, gave a good dacent blast that soon roused them. 'Are yees asleep?' says he, when they awoke. 'Why, then, bud-an-age!' says he, 'isn't it a burning shame for able stout fellows like yees to be asleep at the hour o' midnight of all hours o' the

---

[1] *Shud urth* is an Irish salutation or toast (see Glossary). Darby means Shadrach, Meshach, and Abednego, who were unharmed by the fiery furnace.—ED.

night. Tare-an-age!' says he, 'get up wid yees, you dirty *spalpeens!* There's St. Pathrick in Jerooslem beyant; the Pope's signin' his mittimus to Ireland, to bless it in regard that neither corn, nor barley, nor phaties will grow an the land in consequence of a set of varmint that ates it up; an' there's not a glass o' whisky to be had in Ireland for love or money,' says Lucifer. 'Get up wid yees,' says he, 'an' go in an' get his blessin'; sure, there's not a Catholic in the counthry, barrin' Swaddlers,[1] but's in the town by this,' says he; 'ay, an' many o' the Protestants themselves, and the "black-mouths,"[2] an' "blue-bellies" are gone in to get a share of it. And now,' says he, 'bekase you wor so heavy-headed, I ordher it from this out, that the present night is to be obsarved in the Catholic Church all over the world, an' must be kep holy; an' no thrue Catholic ever will miss from this pariod an opportunity of bein' awake at midnight,' says he, 'glory be to God!' An' now, good Christians, you have an account o' the blessed carol I was singin' for yees. They're but hapuns apiece; an' anybody that has the grace to keep one o' these about them will never meet wid sudden deaths or accidents, sich as hangin', or drownin', or bein' taken suddenly wid a configuration inwardly. I wanst knew a holy man that had a dhrame—about a friend of his it was—will any of yees take one? Thank you, *a colleen*—my blessin', the blessin' o' the pilgrim be an you! God bless you, Mike Reillaghan; an' I'm proud that he put it into your heart to buy one, for the rasons you know. An' now that Father Hoolaghan's comin', any of yees that 'ill want them 'ill find me here agin when mass is over—Oxis Doxis Glorioxis, Amin!"

The priest at this time made his appearance, and those who had been assembled on the cross-roads joined the crowd at the chapel. No sooner was it bruited among them that their pastor had arrived, than the noise, gabble, singing, and laughing were immediately hushed; the shebeen and public houses were left untenanted; and all flocked to the chapel green, where mass was to be said, as the crowd was too large to be contained within the small chapel.

---

[1] Perverts from Catholicity.   [2] Presbyterians.

Mike Reillaghan and Peggy Gartland were among the last who sought the "green;" as lovers they probably preferred walking apart, to the inconvenience of being jostled by the multitude. As they sauntered on slowly after the rest, Mike felt himself touched on the shoulder, and on turning round found Darby More beside him.

"It's painful to my feelins," observed the mendicant, "to have to say this blessed night that your father's son should act so shabby an' ondacent."

"Saints above! how, Darby?"

"Why, don't you know that only for me—for what I heard, an' what I tould you—you'd not have the purty girl here at your elbow? Wasn't it, as I said, his intintion to come an' whip up the *colleen* to Kilnaheery while the family ud be at mass? Sure, only for this, I say, you *bosthoon*, an' that I made you bring her to mass, where ud the purty *colleen* be?—why, half-way to Kilnaheery, an' the girl disgraced for ever!"

"Thrue for you, Darby, I grant it; but what do you want me to do?"

"Oh, for that matther, nothin' at all, Mike; only I suppose that when your tailor made the clothes an you he put no pockets to them?"

"Oh, I see where you are, Darby! Well, here's a crown for you; an' when Peggy an' I's made man an' wife you'll get another."

"Mike, *achora*, I see you are your father's son still. Now listen to me. First, you needn't fear sudden death while you keep that blessed carol about you. Next, get your friends together goin' home, for Frank might jist take the liberty, wid about a score of his 'boys,' to lift her from you even thin. Do the thing I say—don't thrust him; an', moreover, watch in her father's house to-night wid your friends. Thirdly, make it up wid Frank; there's an oath upon you both, you persave. Make it up wid him, if he axes you: don't have a broken oath upon you; for if you refuse he'll get you put out o' connection,[1] and that ud plase him to the backbone."

Mike felt the truth and shrewdness of this advice, and

---

[1] Expel him.

111

determined to follow it. Both young men had been members of an illegal society, and in yielding to their passions so far as to assault each other, had been guilty of bad faith. The following Christmas Day had been appointed by their parish delegates to take the quarrel into consideration; and the best means of escaping censure was certainly to express regret for what had occurred, and to terminate the hostility by an amicable adjustment of their disputes.

They had now reached the chapel green, where the scene that presented itself was so striking and strange that we will give the reader an imperfect sketch of its appearance. He who stood at midnight upon a little mount which rose behind the chapel might see between five and six thousand torches, all blazing together, and forming a level mass of red, dusky light, burning against the dark horizon. These torches were so close to each other that their light seemed to blend, as if they had constituted one wide surface of flame; and nothing could be more preternatural - looking than the strikingly devotional countenances of those who were assembled at their midnight worship, when observed beneath this canopy of fire. The mass was performed under the open sky, upon a table covered with the sacrificial linen and other apparatus for the ceremony. The priest stood, robed in white, with two large torches on each side of his book, reciting the prayers in a low, rapid voice, his hands raised, whilst the congregation were hushed and bent forward in the reverential silence of devotion, their faces touched by the strong blaze of the torches into an expression of deep solemnity. The scenery about the place was wild and striking; and the stars, scattered thinly over the heavens, twinkled with a faint religious light that blended well with the solemnity of this extraordinary worship, and rendered the rugged nature of the abrupt cliffs and precipices, together with the still out-line of the stern mountains, sufficiently visible to add to the wildness and singularity of the ceremony. In fact, there was an unearthly character about it; and the spectre-like appearance of the white-robed priest, as he

" Muttered his prayer to the midnight air,"

would almost impress a man with the belief that it was a

meeting of the dead, and that the priest was repeating, like the Grey Friar, his

"Mass of the days that were gone."

On the ceremony being concluded, the scene, however, was instantly changed: the lights were waved and scattered promiscuously among each other, giving an idea of confusion and hurry that was strongly contrasted with the death-like stillness that prevailed a few minutes before. The gabble and laugh were again heard loud and hearty, and the public and shebeen houses once more became crowded. Many of the young people made, on these occasions, what is called "a run-away;" [1] and other peccadilloes took place, for which the delinquents were either "read out from the altar," or sent probably to St. Patrick's Purgatory at Lough Derg to do penance. Those who did not choose to stop in the whisky houses now hurried home with all speed, to take some sleep before early mass, which was to be performed the next morning about daybreak. The same number of lights might therefore be seen streaming in different ways over the parish; the married men holding the torches, and leading their wives; bachelors escorting their sweethearts, and not unfrequently extinguishing their flambeaux, that the dependence of the females upon their care and protection might more lovingly call forth their gallantry.

When Mike Reillaghan considered with due attention the hint which Darby More had given him touching the necessity of collecting his friends as an escort for Peggy Gartland, he had strong reasons to admit its justness and propriety. After mass he spoke to about two dozen young fellows, who joined him, and under their protection Peggy now returned safely to her father's house.

Frank M'Kenna and his wife reached home about two o'clock; the dance was comparatively thin, though still kept up with considerable spirit. Having solemnised himself by the grace of so sacred a rite, Frank thought proper to close the amusement, and recommend those whom he found in the barn to return to their respective dwellings.

---

[1] Rustic elopement.

"You have had a merry night, childher," said he; "but too much o' one thing's good for nothin'; so don't make a toil of a pleasure, but go all home dacently an' soberly, in the name o' God."

This advice was accordingly followed. The youngsters separated, and M'Kenna joined his family, "to have a sup along wid the man Barny, in honour of what they had hard." It was upon this occasion he missed his son Frank, whose absence from the dance he had not noticed since his return until then.

"*Musha*, where's Frank?" he inquired. "I'll warrant him away wid his blackguards upon no good. God look down upon him! Many a black heart has that boy left us! If it's not the will o' Heaven, I fear he'll come to no good. Barny, is he long gone from the dance?"

"Throth, Frank, wid the noise an' dancin', an' me bein' *dark*," replied Barny shrewdly, "I can't take an me to say. For all you spake agin him, the sorra one of him but's a clane, dacent, spirited boy as there is widin a great ways of him. Here's all your healths! Faix, girls, you'll all sleep sound to-night."

"Well," said Mrs. M'Kenna, "the knowledge of that Darby More is onknowable! Here's a carol I bought from him, an' if you wor but to hear the explanations he put to it! Why, Father Hoolaghan could hardly outdo him!"

"Divil a man in the five parishes can dance 'Jig Polthogue' wid him, for all that," said Barny. "Many a time *Granua* an' I played it for him, an' you'd know the tune upon his feet. He undherstands a power o' *ranns* an' prayers, an' has charms an' holy herbs for all kinds of ailments, no doubt."

"These men, you see," observed Mrs. M'Kenna, in the true spirit of credulity and superstition, "may do many things that the likes of us oughtn't to do, by rason of their great fastin' an' prayin'."

"Thrue for you, Alley," replied her husband; "but come, let us have a sup more in comfort. The sleep's gone *a shaughran* an us this night, anyway; so, Barny, give us a song, an' afther that we'll have a taste o' prayers, to close the night."

"But you don't think of the long journey I've before me,"

114

replied Barny; "how-and-iver, if you promise to send some one home wid me, we'll have the song. I wouldn't care, but the night bein' dark, you see, I'll want somebody to guide me."

"Faith, an' it's but rasonable, Barny, an' you must get Rody home wid you. I suppose he's asleep in his bed by this, but we'll rouse him."

Barny replied by a loud triumphant laugh, for this was one of his standing jests.

"Well, Frank," said he, "I never thought you war so soft, an' me can pick my steps the same at night as in daylight. Sure, that's the way I done them to-night when one o' *Granua's* strings broke. 'Sweets o' rosin!' says I; 'a candle —bring me a candle immedintly.' An' down came Rody in all haste wid a candle. 'Six eggs to you, Rody,' says myself, ' an' half a dozen o' them rotten! but you're a bright boy to bring a lit candle to a blind man!' and then he stood a *bauliore* to the whole house—ha, ha, ha!"

Barny, who was not the man to rise first from the whisky, commenced the relation of his choicest anecdotes. Old Frank and the family, being now in a truly genial mood, entered into the spirit of his jests; so that between chat, songs, and whisky, the hour had now advanced to four o'clock. The fiddler was commencing another song, when the door opened, and Frank presented himself nearly, but not altogether, in a state of intoxication; his face was besmeared with blood; and his whole appearance that of a man under the influence of strong passion, such as would seem to be produced by disappointment and defeat.

"What!" said the father; "is it snowin', Frank? Your clothes are covered wid snow!"

"Lord, guard us!" exclaimed the mother; "is that blood upon your face, Frank?"

"It is snowin', and it is blood that's upon my face," answered Frank moodily. "Do you want to know more news?"

"Why, ay indeed," replied his mother, "we want to hear how you came to be cut!"

"You won't hear it, then," he replied.

The mother was silent, for she knew the terrible fits of passion to which he was subject.

The father groaned deeply, and exclaimed, "Frank, Frank,

God help you, an' show you the sins you're committin', an' the heart-scaldin' you're givin' both your mother an' me! What fresh scrimmage had you that you're in that state?"

"Spare yourself the throuble of inquirin'," he replied; "all I can say," he continued, starting up into sudden fury—"all I can say—an' I say it—I swear it—where's the prayer-book?" and he ran frantically to a shelf beside the dresser on which the prayer-book lay—"ay! by Him that made me I'll swear it—by this sacred book, while I live, Mike Reillaghan, the husband of Peggy Gartland you'll never be, if I should swing for it! Now you all seen I kissed the book!" As he spoke he tossed it back upon the shelf.

The mirth that had prevailed in the family was immediately hushed, and a dead silence ensued. Frank sat down, but instantly rose again, and flung the chair from him with such violence that it was crashed to pieces; he muttered oaths and curses, ground his teeth, and betrayed all the symptoms of jealousy, hatred, and disappointment.

"Frank, *a bouchal*," said Barny, commencing to address him in a conciliatory tone—"Frank, man alive——"

"Hould your tongue, I say, you blind vagabone, or, by the night above us, I'll break your fiddle over your skull if you dare to say another word. What I swore I'll do, an' let no one crass me."

He was a powerful young man, and such was his temper, and so well was it understood, that not one of the family durst venture a word of remonstrance.

The father rose, went to the door, and returned. "Barny," said he, "you must contint yourself where you are for this night. It's snowin' heavily, so you had betther sleep wid Rody; I see a light in the barn; I suppose he's afther bringin' in his bed an' makin' it."

"I'll do anything," replied the poor fiddler, now apprehensive of violence from the outrageous temper of young Frank.

"Well, thin," added the good man, "let us all go to bed, in the name of God. Micaul, bring Barny to the barn, and see that he's comfortable."

This was complied with, and the family quietly and timidly retired to rest, leaving the violent young man storming and digesting his passion behind them.

Mass on Christmas morning was then, as now, performed at daybreak, and again the Roman Catholic inhabitants of the parish were up betimes to attend it. Frank M'Kenna's family were assembled, notwithstanding their short sleep, at an early breakfast; but their meal, in consequence of the unpleasant sensation produced by the outrage of their son, was less cheerful than it would otherwise have been. Perhaps, too, the gloom which hung over them was increased by the snow that had fallen the night before, and by the wintry character of the day, which was such as to mar much of their expected enjoyment. There was no allusion made to their son's violence overnight; neither did he himself appear to be in any degree affected by it. When breakfast was over they prepared to attend mass, and, what was unusual, young Frank was the first to set out for the chapel.

"Maybe," said the father, after he was gone—"maybe that fool of a boy is sarry for his behaviour. It's many a day since I knew him to go to mass of his own accord. It's a good sign, anyway."

"*Musha*," inquired his mother, "what could happen atween him and that civil boy, Mike Reillaghan?"

"The sorra one o' me knows," replied his father; "an' now that I think of it, sure enough there was none o' them at the dance last night, although I sent himself down for them. Micaul," he added, addressing the other son, "will you put an your big coat, slip down to Reillaghan's, an' bring me word what came atween them at all; an' tell Owen himself the thruth, that this boy's breakin' our hearts by his coorses."

Micaul, who, although he knew the cause of the enmity between these rivals, was ignorant of that which occasioned his brother's rash oath, also felt anxious to ascertain the circumstances of the last quarrel. For this purpose, as well as in obedience to his father's wishes, he proceeded to Reillaghan's, and arrived just as Darby More and young Mike had set out for mass.

"What," said the mendicant, "can be bringin' Micaul down, I wondher? Somethin' about that slip o' grace, his brother."

"I suppose so," said Mike; "an' I wish the same slip was as dacent an' inoffensive as he is. I don't know a boy livin'

117

I'd go farther for nor the same Micaul. He's a credit to the family as much as the other's a stain upon them."

"Well, anyhow, you war Frank's match, an' more, last night. How bitther he was bint on bringin' Peggy aff, when he an' his set waited till they seen the country clear, an' thought the family asleep! Had you man for man, Mike?"

"Ay, about that; an' we set so snug in Peggy's that you'd hear a pin fallin'. A hard tug, too, there was in the beginnin'; but whin they found that we had a strong back they made away, an' we gave them purshute from about the house."

"You may thank me, anyhow, for havin' her to the good; but I knew by my dhrame, wid the help o' God, that there was somethin' to happen—by the same a-token that your mother's an the high horse about that dhrame. I'm to tell it to her, wid the sinse of it, in the evenin', when the day's past, an' all of us in comfort."

"What was it, Darby? Sure, you may let me hear it."

"Maybe I will in the evenin'. It was about you an' Peggy, the darlin'. But how will you manage in regard of breakin' the oath and sthrikin' a brother?"

"Why, that I couldn't get over it whin he struck me first. Sure, he's worse off. I'll lave it to the Diligates, an' whatever judgment they give out I'll take wid it."

"Well," observed Darby sarcastically, "it made him do one good turn, anyway."

"What was that, Darby? for good turns are but scarce wid him."

"Why, it made him hear mass to-day," replied the mendicant; "an' that's what he hadn't the grace to do this many a year. It's away in the mountains wid his gun he'd be thracin', an' a fine day it is for it—only this business prevints him. Now, Mike," observed Darby, "as we're comin' out upon the *boreen*, I'll fall back, an' do you go an. I have part of my *padareens* to say, before I get to the chapel, wid a blessin'; an' we had as good not be seen together."

The mendicant, as he spoke, pulled out a long pair of beads, on which he commenced his prayers, occasionally accosting an acquaintance with a *gho mhany Deah ghud*, and sometimes taking a part in the conversation for a minute or two, after which he resumed the prayers as before.

The day was now brightening up, although the earlier part of the morning had threatened severe weather. Multitudes were flocking to the chapel; the men well secured in frieze greatcoats, in addition to which many of them had their legs bound with straw ropes, and others with leggings made of old hats cut up for the purpose. The women were secured with cloaks, the hoods of which were tied with kerchiefs of some showy colour over their bonnets or their caps, which, together with their elbows projecting behind, for the purpose of preventing their dress from being dabbled in the snow, gave them a marked and most picturesque appearance.

Reillaghan and M'Kenna both reached the chapel a considerable time before the arrival of the priest; and as a kind of Whiteboy committee was to sit for the purpose of investigating their conduct in holding out so dangerous an example as they did by striking each other, contrary to their oaths as brothers under the same system, they accordingly were occupied each in collecting his friends, and conciliating those whom they supposed to be hostile to them on the opposite party. It had been previously arranged that this committee should hold a court of inquiry, and that provided they could not agree, the matter was to be referred to two hedge schoolmasters, who should act as umpires; but if it happened that the latter could not decide it, there was no other tribunal appointed to which a final appeal could be made.

According to these regulations a court was opened in a *shebeen*-house that stood somewhat distant from the road. Twelve young fellows seated themselves on each side of a deal table, with one of the umpires at each end of it, and a bottle of whisky in the middle. In a higher sphere of life it is usual to refer such questionable conduct as occurs in duelling to the arbitration of those who are known to be qualified by experience in the duello. On this occasion the practice was not departed from, those who had been thus selected as the committee being the most notoriously pugnacious "boys" in the whole parish.

"Now, boys," said one of the schoolmasters, "let us proceed to operations wid proper spirit," and he filled a glass

119

of whisky as he spoke. "Here's all your healths; and next, pace and unanimity to us! Call in the culprits."

Both were accordingly admitted, and the first speaker resumed: "Now, in the second place, I'll read yees that part o' the oath which binds us all under the obligation of not strikin' one another—hem! hem!—'No brother is to strike another, knowing him to be such; he's to strike him —hem!—neither in fair nor market, at home nor abroad, neither in public nor in private, neither on Sunday nor week-day, present or absent, nor——"

"I condimn that," observed the other master. "I condimn it, as bein' too latitudinarian in principle, an' containing a paradogma; besides, it's bad grammar."

"You're rather airly in the market wid your bad grammar," replied the other. "I'll grant you the paradogma, but I'll stand up for the grammar of it while I'm able to stand up for anything."

"Faith, an' if you rise to stand up for that," replied his friend, "and doesn't choose to sit down till you prove it to be good grammar, you'll be a standin' joke all your life."

"I bleeve it's purty conspicuous in the parish that I have often, in our disputations about grammar, left you widout a leg to stand upon at all," replied the other.

This sally was well received, but his opponent was determined to push home the argument at once.

"I would be glad to know," he inquired, "by what beauti-ful invintion a man could contrive to strike another in his absence? Have you good grammar for that?"

"And did you never hear of detraction?" replied his opponent—"that is, a man who's in the habit of spaking falsehoods of his friends whin their backs are turned, that is to say, whin they are absent. Now, sure, if a man's absent whin his back's turned, mayn't any man whose back's turned be said to be absent; ergo, to strike a man behind his back is to strike him whin he's absent. Does that confound you? Where's your logic and grammar to meet proper ratiocination like what I'm displaying?"

"Faith," replied the other, "you may have had logic and grammar, but I'll take my oath it was in your younger years, for both have been absent ever since I knew you: they turned their backs upon you, man alive; for they didn't like, you see, to be keepin' bad company—ha, ha, ha!"

"Why, you poor crathur," said his antagonist, "if I choose to let myself out, I'd make a hare of you in no time, entirely."

"And an ass of yourself," retorted the other; "but you may save yourself the throuble in regard of the last, for your frinds know you to be an ass ever since they remimber you. You have them here, man alive—the auricles," and he pointed to his ears.

"Hut! get out wid you, you poor Jamaica-headed castigator, you; sure, you never had more nor a thimbleful o' sinse on any subject."

"Faith, an' the thimble that measured yours was a tailor's one widout a bottom in it, an' good measure you got, you miserable flagellator! what are you but a *nux vomica!* A fit o' the ague's a thrifle compared to your asinity."

The "boys" were delighted at this encounter, and utterly forgetful of the pacific occasion on which they had assembled, began to pit them against each other with great glee.

"That's a hard hit, Misther Costigan; but you won't let it pass, anyhow."

"The ague an' you are ould acquaintances," retorted Costigan; "whenever a scrimmage takes place, you're sure to resave a visit from it."

"Why, I'm not such a haro as yourself," replied his rival, "nor such a great hand at batin' the absent!"

"Bravo, Misther Connell! that's a leveller. Come, Misther Costigan, bedad, if you don't answer that you're bate."

"By this and by that, man alive, if you don't mend your manners, maybe I'd make it betther for you to be absent also. You'll only put me to the throuble of mendin' them for you."

"Mend my manners!" exclaimed his opponent, with a bitter sneer — "you to mend them! Out wid your budget and your hammer, then. You're the very tinker of good manners—bekase for one dacency you'd mend, you'd spoil twenty."

"I'm able to hammer you, at all events, or, for that matther, any one of your illiterate gineration. Sure, it's

121

well known that you can't tache Vosther[1] widout the kay."

"Hould there, if you plase," exclaimed one of his opponent's relations; "don't lug in his family; that's known to be somewhat afore your own, I bleeve. There's no informers among them, Misther Costigan — keep at home, masther, if you plase."

"At home! that's more than some o' your own *cleaveens* have been able to do," rejoined Costigan, alluding to one of the young fellow's acquaintances who had been transported.

"Do you mane to put an affront upon me?" said the other.

"Since the *barrhad* fits you, wear it," replied Costigan.

"Very right, masther, make him a present of it," exclaimed one of Costigan's distant relations; "he desarves that, an' more if he'd get it."

"Do I?" said the other. "An' what have *you* to say on the head of it?"

"Why, not much," answered Bartle, "only that you ought to've left it betune them; an' that *I'll* back Misther Costigan agin any rascal that ud say there was ever a drop of his blood in an informer's veins."

"*I* say it, for one," replied the other.

"And I, for another," said Connell; "an', what's worse, I'll hould a wager that if he was searched this minute you'd find a kay to Gough in his pocket, although he throws Vosther in my teeth—the dunce never goes widout one. Sure, he's not able to set a dacent copy, or headline, or to make a dacent hook, nor a hanger, nor a down-stroke, and was a poor scholar, too!"

"I'll give you a down-stroke in the manetime, you ignoramus," said the pedagogue, throwing himself to the end of the table at which his enemy sat, and laying him along the floor by a single blow.

He was instantly attacked by the friend of the prostrate academician, who was in his turn attacked by the friend of Costigan. The adherents of the respective teachers were

---

[1] Elias Voster's " Arithmetic " was the only serious rival to Gough's in Ireland at this time. —ED.

122

immediately rushing to a general engagement, when the door opened, and Darby More made his appearance.

"Asy!—stop wid yees!—hould back, ye disgraceful villains!" exclaimed the mendicant, in a thundering voice—"be asy, I say. Saints in glory! is this the way you're settling the dispute between the two dacent young men, that's sorry, both o' them, I'll go bail, for what they done. Sit down, every one of yees, or, by the blessed ordhers I wear about me, I'll report yees to Father Hoolaghan, an' have yees read out from the althar, or sint to Lough Derg! Sit down I say!"

As he spoke he extended his huge cant between the hostile parties, and thrust them one by one to their seats with such muscular energy that he had them sitting before another blow could be given.

"Saints in glory!" he exclaimed again, "isn't this blessed doins an the sacred day that's in it, that a poor, helpless ould man like me can't come to get somethin' to take away this misfortunit touch o' configuration that I'm afflicted wid in cowld weather—that I can't take a little sup of the only thing that cures me, widout your ructions and battles! You came here to make pace between two dacent men's childher, and you're as bad, if not worse, yourselves. Oh, *wurrah dheelish*, what's this! I'm in downright agony! Oh, murdher *sheery!* Has none o' yees a hand to thry if there's e'er a dhrop of relief in that bottle? or am I to die all out, in the face o' the world, for want of a sup o' something to warm me?"

"Darby, thry the horn," said M'Kenna.

"Here, Darby," said one of them, "dhrink this off, an' my life for yours, it'll warm you to the marrow!"

"Och, *musha*, but I wanted it badly," replied Darby, swallowing it at once; "it's the only thing does me good when I'm this way. *Dhea grasthias!* [1] Oxis Doxis Glorioxis, Amin!"

"I think," said M'Kenna, "that what's in the horn's far afore it."

"Oh, thin, you thoughtless crathur, if you knew somethin' I hard about you a while ago, you'd think otherwise. But

---

[1] *Deo gratias.*

indeed it's thrue for you; I'm sure I'd be sarry to compare what's in it to anything o' the kind I tuck. *Dhea grasthias!* throth, I'm asier now a great dale nor I was."

"Will you take another sup, Darby?" inquired the young fellow in whose hands the bottle was now nearly empty; "there's jist about another glass."

"Indeed an' I will, *a villish!* an' sure you'll have my blessin' for it, and barrin' the priest's own, you couldn't have a more luckier one, blessed be God for it—sure, that's well known. In throth, they never came to ill that had it, an' never did good that got my curse! Houp!—do you hear how that rises the wind off my stomach? Houp!—*Dhea grasthias* for that!"

"How did you larn all the prayers an' charms you have, Darby?" inquired the bottle-holder.

"It would take me too long to tell you that, *a villish!* But, childher, now that you're all together, make it up wid one another. Aren't you all frinds an' brothers, sworn brothers, an' why would you be fightin' among other? Misther Costigan, give me your hand; sure, I heard a thrifle o' what you were sayin' while I was suckin' my *dudeen* at the fire widout. Come here, Misther Connell. Now, before the saints in glory, I lay my bitther curse an him that refuses to shake hands wid his inimy. There now—I'm proud to see it. Mike, *avourneen*, come here—Frank M'Kenna, *gutsho*, walk over here; my bitther heart's curse upon both of yees if you don't make up all quarrels this minnit! Are you willin', Mike Reillaghan?"

"I have no objection in life," replied Mike, "if he'll say that Peggy Gartland won't be put to any more throuble through his manes."

"There's my hand, Mike," said Frank, "that I forget an' forgive all that's past; an' in regard o' Peggy Gartland, why, as she's so dark agin me, I lave her to you for good."

"Well! see what it is to have the good intintions!—to be makin' pace an' friendship atween inimies! That's all I think about, an' nothin' gives me greater pleas——— Saints o' glory!—what's this!—oh, *wurrah!*—that thief of a—*wurrah dheelish!*—that touch o' configuration's comin' back agin!—oh, thin, but it's hard to get it undher!—oh!———"

"I'm sarry for it, Darby," replied he who held the now empty bottle, "for the whisky's out."

"Throth, and I'm sarry myself, for nothin' else does me good; an' Father Hoolaghan says nothin' can keep it down, barrin' the sup o' whisky. It's best burnt wid a little bit o' butther an it; but I can't get that always, it overtakes me so suddenly. Glory be to God!"

"Well," said M'Kenna, "as Mike an' myself was the manes of bringin' us together, why, if he joins me, we'll have another bottle."

"Throth, an' it's fair an' dacent, an' he must do it; by the same a-token, that I'll not lave the house till it's dhrunk, for there's no thrustin' yees together, you're so hot-headed an' ready to rise the hand," said Darby.

M'Kenna and Mike, having been reconciled, appeared in a short time warmer friends than ever. While the last bottle went round, those who had before been on the point of engaging in personal conflict now laughed at their own foibles, and expressed the kindness and goodwill which they felt for each other at heart.

"Now," said the mendicant, "go all of you to mass, an' as soon as you can to confission, for it's not good to have the broken oath an' the sin of it over one. Confiss it, an' have your consciences light; sure, it's a happiness that you can have the guilt taken off o' yees, childher."

"Thrue for you, Darby," they replied; "an' we'll be thinkin' of your advice."

"Ay, do, childher; an' there's Father Hoolaghan comin' down the road, so, in the name o' goodness, we haven't a minnit to lose."

They all left the shebeen-house as he spoke, except Frank and himself, who remained until they had gone out of hearing.

"Darby," said he, "I want you to come up to our house in the mornin', an' bring along wid you the things that you stamp the crass upon the skin wid; I'm goin' to get the crucifix put upon me; but, on the paril o' your life, don't brathe a word of it to mortual."

"God enable you, *avick!* it's a good intintion. I will indeed be up wid you—airly, too, wid a blessin'. It is that, indeed—a good intintion, sure enough."

The parish chapel was about one hundred perches from the shebeen-house in which the "boys" had assembled; the latter were proceeding there in a body when Frank overtook them.

"Mike," said he, aside to Reillaghan, "we'll have time enough—walk back a bit. I'll tell you what I'm thinkin'; you never seen in your life a finer day for thracin'; what ud you say if we give the boys the slip, never heed mass, an' set off to the mountains?"

"Won't we have time enough afther mass?" said Reillaghan.

"Why, man, sure, you did hear mass once to-day. Weren't you at it last night? No, indeed, we won't be time enough afther it; for this bein' Chris'mas day, we must be home at dinner-time—you know it's not lucky to be from the family upon set days. Hang-an-ounty, come; we'll have fine sport; I have cock-sticks[1] enough. The best part of the day'll be gone if we wait for mass. Come, an' let us start."

"Well, well," replied Reillaghan, "the sarra hair I care; so let us go. I'd like myself to have a rap at the hares in the Black Hills, sure enough; but as it ud be remarkable for us to be seen lavin' mass, why, let us crass the field here, an' get out upon the road above the bridge."

To this his companion assented, and they both proceeded at a brisk pace, each apparently anxious for the sport, and resolved to exhibit such a frank cordiality of manner as might convince the other that all their past enmity was forgotten and forgiven.

Their direct path to the mountains lay by M'Kenna's house, where it was necessary they should call, in order to furnish themselves with cock-sticks and to bring dogs, which young Frank kept for the purpose. The inmates of the family were at mass, with the exception of Frank's mother, and Rody, the servant man, whom they found sitting on his own bed in the barn, engaged at cards, the right hand against the left.

"Well, Rody," said Frank, "who's winnin'?"

---

[1] A stick which was thrown at a cock tied to a stake, a game practised by the people on a day known as "Cock-Monday."—ED.

"The left entirely," replied his companion; "the divil a game at all the right's gettin', whatever's the rason of it, an' I'm always turnin' up black. I hope none of my frinds or acquaintances will die soon."

"Throw them aside—quit of them," said Frank; "give them to me, I'll put them past, an' do you bring us out the gun. I've the powdher an' shot here; we may as well bring her, an' have a slap at them. One o' the officers in the barracks of —— keeps me in powdher an' shot, besides givin' me an odd crown, an' I keep him in game."

"Why, thin, boys," observed Rody, "what's the manin' o' this?—two o' the biggest inimies in Europe last night an' this mornin', an' now as great as two thieves! How does that come?"

"Very asy, Rody," replied Reillaghan; "we made up the quarrel, shuck hands, an's good frinds as ever."

"Bedad, that bates cock-fightin'," said Rody, as he went to bring in the gun.

In the meantime, Frank, with the cards in his hand, went to the eave of the barn, thrust them up under the thatch, and took out of the same nook a flask of whisky.

"We'll want this," said he, putting it to his lips and gulping down a portion. "Come, Mike, be tastin'; an' afther-wards put this in your pocket."

Mike followed his example, and was corking the flask when Rody returned with the gun.

"She's charged," said Frank; "but we'd betther put in fresh primin' for fraid of her hangin' fire."

He then primed the gun, and handed it to Reillaghan. "Do you keep the gun, Mike," he added, "an' I'll keep the cock-sticks. Rody, I'll bet you a shillin' I kill more wid a cock-stick nor he will wid the gun. Will you take me up?"

"I know a safer thrick," replied Rody. "You're a dead aim wid the cock-stick, sure enough, an' a deader aim wid the gun, too—catch me at it."

"You show some sinse, for a wondher," observed Frank, as he and his companion left the barn, and turned towards the mountain, which rose frowning behind the house.

Rody stood looking after them until they wound up slowly out of sight among the hills; he then shook his head two or three times, and exclaimed, "By dad, there's somethin' in this, if one could make out what it is. I know Frank."

Christmas Day passed among the peasantry as it usually passes in Ireland. Friends met before dinner in their own, in their neighbours', in shebeen or in public houses, where they drank, sang, or fought, according to their natural dispositions, or the quantity of liquor they had taken. The festivity of the day might be known by the unusual reek of smoke that danced from each chimney, by the number of persons who crowded the roads by their brand-new dresses —for if a young man or country girl can afford a dress at all, they provide it for Christmas—and by the striking appearance of those who, having drunk a little too much, were staggering home in the purest happiness, singing, stopping their friends, shaking hands with them, or kissing them without any regard to sex. Many a time might be seen two Irishmen, who had got drunk together, leaving a fair or market, their arms about each other's necks, from whence they only removed them to kiss and hug one another the more lovingly. Notwithstanding this, there is nothing more probable than that these identical two will enjoy the luxury of a mutual battle, by way of episode, and again proceed on their way, kissing and hugging as if nothing had happened to interrupt their friendship. All the usual effects of jollity and violence, fun and fighting, love and liquor, were, of course, to be seen, felt, heard, and understood on this day, in a manner much more remarkable than on common occasions; for it may be observed that the national festivals of the Irish bring out their strongest points of character with peculiar distinctness.

The family of Frank M'Kenna were sitting down to their Christmas dinner; the good man had besought a blessing upon the comfortable and abundant fare of which they were about to partake, and nothing was amiss, save the absence of their younger son.

"*Musha*, where on earth can this boy be stayin'?" said the father. "I'm sure this above all days in the year is one he oughtn't to be from home an."

The mother was about to inform him of the son's having gone to the mountains, when the latter returned, breathless, pale, and horror-struck.

Rody eyed him keenly, and laid down the bit he was conveying to his mouth.

"Heavens above us!" exclaimed his mother, "what ails you?"

He only replied by dashing his hat on the ground, and exclaiming, "Up wid yees!—up wid yees!—quit your dinners! Oh, Rody! what'll be done? Go down to Owen Reillaghan's —go 'way—go down—and tell thim—oh, *vick-na-hoie!* but this was the unfortunate day to us all! Mike Reillaghan is shot wid my gun; she went off in his hand goin' over a snow wreath, an' he's lying dead in the mountains!"

The screams and the wailings which immediately rose in the family were dreadful. Mrs. M'Kenna almost fainted; and the father, after many struggles to maintain his firmness, burst into the bitter tears of disconsolation and affliction. Rody was 'calmer, but turned his eyes from one to another with a look of deep compassion, and again eyed Frank keenly and suspiciously.

Frank's eye caught his, and the glance which had surveyed him with such scrutiny did not escape his observation. "Rody," said he, "do you go an' break it to the Reillaghans: you're the best to do it; for, when we were settin' out, you saw that he carried the gun, an' not me."

"Thrue for you," said Rody; "I saw that, Frank, and can swear to it; but that's all I did see. I know nothing of what happened in the mountains."

"*Damnho seery orth!* What do you mane, you villain?" exclaimed Frank, seizing the tongs, and attempting to strike him. "Do you dar to suspect that I had any hand in it?"

"*Wurrah dheelish,* Frank!" screamed the sisters, "are you goin' to murdher Rody?"

"Murdher!" he shouted, in a paroxysm of fury; "why, the curse o' God upon you all, what puts murdher into your heads? Is it my own family that's the first to charge me wid it?"

"Why, there's no one chargin' you wid it," replied Rody— "not one. Whatever makes you take it to yourself?"

"An' what did you look at me for, thin, the way you did? What did you look at me for, I say?"

"Is it any wondher," replied the servant coolly, "when you had sich a dreadful story to tell?"

"Go off," replied Frank, now hoarse with passion—"go off, an' tell the Reillaghans what happened; but, by all the books that ever was opened or shut, if you breathe a word about murdh—about—if you do, you villain, I'll be the death o' you!"

When Rody was gone on this melancholy errand, old M'Kenna first put the tongs, and everything he feared might be used as a weapon by his frantic son, out of his reach; he then took down the book on which he had the night before sworn so rash and mysterious an oath, and desired the son to look upon it.

"Frank," said he solemnly, "you swore on that blessed book last night that Mike Reillaghan never would be the husband of Peggy Gartland—he's a corpse to-day! Yes," he continued, "the good, the honest, the industrious boy is—" his sobs became so loud and thick that he appeared almost suffocated. "Oh," said he, "may God pity us! As I hope to meet my blessed Saviour, who was born on this day, I would rather you war the corpse, an' not Mike Reillaghan!"

"I don't doubt that," said the son fiercely; "you never showed me much *grah*, sure enough."

"Did you ever desarve it?" replied the father. "Heaven above me knows it was too much kindness was showed you. When you ought to have been well corrected, you got your will an' your way, an' now see the upshot."

"Well," said the son, "it's the last day ever I'll stay in the family; thrate me as bad as you plase. I'll take the king's bounty an' list, if I live to see to-morrow."

"Oh, thin, in the name o' goodness, do so," said the father; "an' so far from previntin' you, we'll bless you when you're gone, for goin'."

"*Arrah*, Frank, *aroon*," said Mrs. M'Kenna, who was now recovered, "maybe, afther all, it was only an accident; sure, we often hard of sich things. Don't you remember Squire Elliott's son, that shot himself by accident, out fowlin'? Frank, can you clear yourself afore us?"

"Oh, Alley! Alley!" exclaimed the father, wiping away his tears, "don't you remember his oath last night?"

"What oath?" inquired the son, with an air of surprise.

130

"what oath last night? I know I was dhrunk last night, but I remimber nothing about an oath."

"Do you deny it, you hardened boy?"

"I do deny it; an' I'm not a hardened boy. What do you all mane? do yees want to dhrive me mad? I know nothin' about any oath last night," replied the son, in a loud voice.

The grief of the mother and daughters was loud during the pauses of the conversation. Micaul, the eldest son, sat beside his father in tears.

"Frank," said he, "many an advice I gave you' between ourselves, and you know how you tuck them. When you'd stale the oats, an' the meal, an' the phaties, an' hay, at night, to have money for your cards an' dhrinkin', I kept it back, an' said nothin' about it. I wish I hadn't done so, for it wasn't for your good; but it was my desire to have as much pace and quietness as possible."

"Frank," said the father, eyeing him solemnly, "it's possible that you do forget the oath you made last night, for you war in liquor; I would give the wide world that it was thrue. Can you now, in the presence of God, clear yourself of havin' act or part in the death of Mike Reillaghan?"

"What ud ail me," said the son, "if I liked?"

"Will you do it now for our satisfaction, an' take a load of misery off of our hearts? It's the laste you may do, if you can do it. In the presence of the great God, will you clear yourself now?"

"I suppose," said the son, "I'll have to clear myself to-morrow, an' there's no use in my doin' it more than wanst. When the time comes I'll do it."

The father put his hands on his eyes, and groaned aloud; so deep was his affliction that the tears trickled through his fingers during this fresh burst of sorrow. The son's refusal to satisfy them renewed the grief of all, as well as of the father; it rose again, louder than before, whilst young Frank sat opposite the door, silent and sullen.

It was now dark, but the night was calm and agreeable. M'Kenna's family felt the keen affliction which we have endeavoured to describe. The dinner was put hastily aside, and the festive spirit peculiar to this night became changed into one of gloom and sorrow. In this state they sat, when the voice of grief was heard loud in the distance—the strong cry of men, broken and abrupt, mingled with the shrieking wail of female lamentation.

The M'Kennas started, and Frank's countenance assumed an expression which it would be difficult to describe. There was, joined to his extreme paleness, a restless, apprehensive, and determined look; each trait apparently struggling for the ascendency in his character, and attempting to stamp his face with its own expression.

"Do you hear that?" said his father. "Oh, *musha*, Father of Heaven, look down an' support that family this night! Frank, if you take my advice you'll lave their sight; for surely if they brained you on the spot who could blame them?"

"Why ought I lave their sight?" replied Frank. "I tell you all that I had no hand in his death. The gun went off by accident as he was crassin' a wreath o' snow. I was afore him, and when I heard the report, an' turned round, there he lay, shot an' bleedin'. I thought it mightn't signify, but on lookin' at him closely I found him quite dead. I then ran home, never touchin' the gun at all, till his family an' the neighbours ud see him. Surely, it's no wondher I'd be distracted in my mind; but that's no rason you should all open upon me, as if I had murdhered the boy!"

"Well," said the father, "I'm glad to hear you say even that much. I hope it may be betther wid you than we all think; an' oh! grant it, sweet Mother o' Heaven, this day! Now carry yourself quietly afore the people. If they abuse you, don't fly into a passion, but make allowance for their grief and misery."

In the meantime the tumult was deepening as it approached M'Kenna's house. The report had almost instantly spread through the village in which Reillaghan lived; and the loud cries of his father and brothers, who, in the wildness of their despair, continually called upon his name, had been heard at the houses which lay scattered over the neighbourhood. Their inmates, on listening to such unusual sounds, sought the direction from which they proceeded; for it was quite evident that some terrible calamity had befallen the Reillaghans in consequence of the son's name being borne on the blasts of night with such loud and overwhelming tones of grief and anguish. The assembly, on reaching M'Kenna's, might therefore be numbered at thirty, including the females of Reillaghan's immediate family, who had been strung by the energy of despair to a capability of bearing any fatigue, or, rather, to an utter insensibility of all bodily suffering.

We must leave the scene which ensued to the reader's imagination, merely observing that as neither the oath which young Frank had taken the preceding night, nor, indeed, the peculiar bitterness of his enmity towards the deceased, was known by the Reillaghans, they did not, therefore, discredit the account of his death which they had heard.

Their grief was exclamatory and full of horror; consisting of prolonged shrieks on the part of the women, and frantic howlings on that of the men. The only words they uttered were his name, with epithets and ejaculations. "*Oh, a Vichaul dheelish—a Vichaul dheelish—a bouchal ban machree—nuill thu marra?— nuill thu marra?*" "Oh, Michael, the beloved— Michael, the beloved—fair boy of our heart—are you dead? —are you dead?"

From M'Kenna's the crowd, at the head of which was Darby More, proceeded towards the mountains, many of them bearing torches, such as had been used on their way to the Midnight Mass. The moon had disappeared, the darkness was deepening, and the sky was overhung with black, heavy clouds, that gave a stormy character to scenery in itself remarkably wild and gloomy.

Young M'Kenna and the pilgrim led them to the dreary waste in which the corpse lay. It was certainly an awful spectacle to behold these unhappy people toiling up the mountain solitude at such an hour, their convulsed faces thrown into striking relief by the light of the torches, and their cries rising in wild, irregular cadences upon the blast which swept over them with a dismal howl, in perfect character with their affliction and the circumstances which produced it.

On arriving within view of the corpse there was a slight pause; for, notwithstanding the dreadful paroxysms of their grief, there was something still more startling and terrible in contemplating the body thus stretched out in the stillness

133

of death on the lonely mountain. The impression it produced was peculiarly solemn: the grief was hushed for a
moment, but only for a moment; it rose again wilder than
before, and in a few minutes the friends of Reillaghan were
about to throw themselves upon the body under the strong
impulse of sorrow and affection.

The mendicant, however, stepped forward. "Hould back,"
said he; "it's hard to ax yees to do it, but still you must.
Let the neighbours about us here examine the body, in
ordher to see whether it mightn't be possible that the dacent
boy came by his death from somebody else's hand than his
own. Hould forrid the lights," said he, "till we see how
he's lyin' an' how the gun's lyin'."

"Darby," said young Frank, "I can't but be oblaged
to you for that. You're the last man livin' ought to say
what you said, afther you seein' us both forget an' forgive
this day. I call upon you now to say whether you didn't
see him an' me shakin' hands, an' buryin' all bad feelin'
between us?"

"I'll spake to you jist now," replied the mendicant. "See
here, neighbours—observe this: the boy was shot in the
breast, an' here's not a snow-wreath, but a *weeshy* dhrift that
a child ud step acrass widout an accident. I tell yees all
that I suspect foul play in this."

"H——'s fire!" exclaimed the brother of the deceased;
"what's that you say? What? Can it be—can it—can it—
that you murdhered him, you villain, that's known to be
nothin' but a villain? But I'll do for you!" He snatched
at the gun as he spoke, and would probably have taken
ample vengeance upon Frank had not the mendicant and
others prevented him.

"Have sinse," said Darby; "this is not the way to behave,
man. Lave the gun lyin' where she is till we see more about
us. Stand back there, an' let me look at these marks—ay,
about five yards—there's the track of feet about five yards
before him—here they turn about an' go back. Here,
Saviour o' the world! see here! the mark, clane an' clear,
of the butt o' the gun! Now, if that boy stretched afore us
had the gun in his hand the time she went off, could the
mark of it be here? Bring me down the gun—an' the curse

o' God upon her for an unlucky thief, whoever had her! It's thrue!—it's too thrue!" he continued—"the man that had the gun stood on this spot!"

"It's a falsity!" said Frank—"it's a damnable falsity! Rody Teague, I call upon you to spake for me. Didn't you see, when we went to the hills, that it was Mike carried the gun, an' not me?"

"I did," replied Rody; "I can swear to that."

"Ay," exclaimed Frank, with triumph, "an' you yourself, Darby, saw us, as I said, makin' up whatsomever little difference there was betwixt us."

"I did," replied the mendicant sternly; "but I heard you say, no longer ago than last night—say! why, you shwore it, man alive!—that if you wouldn't have Peggy Gartland, he never should. In your own stable I heard it, an' I was the manes of disappointing you and your gang when you thought to take away the girl by force. You're well known too often to carry a fair face when the heart under it is black wid you."

"All I can say is," observed young Reillaghan, "that if it comes out agin you that you played him foul, all the earth won't save your life. I'll have your heart's blood, if I should hang for it a thousand times."

This dialogue was frequently interrupted by the sobbings and clamour of the women, and the detached conversation of some of the men, who were communicating to each other their respective opinions upon the melancholy event which had happened.

Darby More now brought Reillaghan's father aside, and thus addressed him :—

"Gluntho!—to tell God's thruth, I've strong suspicions that your son was murdhered. This sacred thing, that I put the crass upon people's breasts wid, saves people from hangin' an' unnatural deaths. Frank spoke to me last night, no longer ago, to come up an' mark it an him to-morrow. My opinion is that he intinded to murdher him at that time, an' wanted to have a protection agin what might happen to him in regard o' the black deed."

"Can we prove it agin him?" inquired the disconsolate father. "I know it'll be hard, as there was no one present but themselves; an' if he did it, surely he'll not confess it."

"We may make him do it, maybe," said the mendicant. "The villain's aisily frightened, an' fond o' charms an' *pishthrogues,* an' sich holy things, for all his wickedness. Don't say a word. We'll take him by surprise. I'll call upon him to TOUCH THE CORPSE. Make them women—an' och, it's hard to expect it—make them stop clappin' their hands an' cryin' ; an' let there be dead silence, if you can."

During this and some other observations made by Darby, Frank had got the gun in his possession, and whilst seeming to be engaged in looking at it and examining the lock, he actually contrived to reload it without having been observed.

"Now, neighbours," said Darby, "hould your tongues for a *weeshy* start, till I ax Frank M'Kenna a question or two. Frank M'Kenna, as you hope to meet God at judgment, did you take his life that's lyin' a corpse before us?"

"I did not," replied M'Kenna; "I could clear myself on all the books in Europe, that he met his death as I tould yees ; an' more nor that," he added, dropping upon his knees and uncovering his head, "MAY I DIE WIDOUT PRIEST OR PRAYER, WIDOUT HELP, HOPE, OR HAPPINESS, UPON THE SPOT WHERE HE'S NOW STRETCHED, IF I MURDHERED OR SHOT HIM."

"I say amin to that," replied Darby. "Oxis Doxis Glorioxis ! So far, that's right, if the blood of him's not an you. But there's one thing more to be done: will you walk over, UNDHER THE EYE OF GOD, AN' TOUCH THE CORPSE? Hould back, neighbours, an' let him come over alone; I an' Owen Reillaghan will stand here wid the lights to see if the corpse bleeds."

"Give me, too, a light," said M'Kenna's father; "my son must get fair play, anyway; I must be a witness myself to it, an' will, too."

"It's but rasonable," said Owen Reillaghan. "Come over beside Darby an' myself; I'm willin' that your son should stand or fall by what'll happen."

Frank's father, with a taper in his hand, immediately went, with a pale face and trembling steps, to the place appointed for him beside the corpse, where he took his stand.

When young M'Kenna heard Darby's last question he seemed as if seized by an inward spasm ; the start which he gave, and his gaspings for breath, were visible to all present.

136

Had he seen the spirit of the murdered man before him his horror could not have been greater; for this ceremony had been considered a most decisive test in cases of suspicion of murder—an ordeal, indeed, to which few murderers wished to submit themselves. In addition to this, we may observe that Darby's knowledge of the young man's character was correct: with all his crimes he was weak-minded and superstitious.

He stood silent for some time after the ordeal had been proposed to him; his hair became literally erect with the dread of this formidable scrutiny, his cheeks turned white, and the cold perspiration fell from him in large drops. All his strength appeared to have departed from him; he stood as if hesitating, and even the energy necessary to stand seemed to be the result of an effort.

"Remember," said Darby, pulling out the large crucifix which was attached to his beads, "that the eye of God is upon you. If you've committed the murdher, thrimble; if not, Frank, you've little to fear in touchin' the corpse."

Frank had not yet uttered a word; but leaning himself on the gun, he looked wildly around him, cast his eyes up to the stormy sky, then turned them with a dead glare upon the corpse and the crucifix.

"Do you confiss the murdher?" said Darby.

"Murdher!" rejoined Frank; "no, I confess no murdher. You villain, do you want to make me guilty? do you want to make me guilty, you deep villain?"

It seemed as if the current of his thoughts and feelings had taken a new direction, though it is probable that the excitement which appeared to be rising within him was only the courage of fear.

"You all wish to find me guilty," he added; "but I'll show yees that I'm not guilty."

He immediately walked towards the corpse, and stooping down, touched the body with one hand, holding the gun in the other. The interest of that moment was intense, and all eyes were strained towards the spot. Behind the corpse, at each shoulder—for the body lay against a small snow wreath, in a recumbent position—stood the father of the deceased and the father of the accused, each wound up by feelings of a directly opposite character to a pitch of dreadful excitement. Over them, in his fantastic dress and white beard, stood the tall mendicant, who held up his crucifix to Frank, with an awful menace upon his strongly-marked countenance. At a little distance to the left of the body stood the other men who were assembled, having their torches held aloft in their hands, and their forms bent towards the corpse, their faces indicating expectation, dread, and horror. The female relations of the deceased stood nearest his remains, their torches extended in the same direction, their visages exhibiting the passions of despair and grief in their wildest characters, but as if arrested by some supernatural object immediately before their eyes that produced a new and more awful feeling than grief. When the body was touched, Frank stood as if himself bound by a spell to the spot. At length he turned his eyes to the mendicant, who stood silent and motionless, with the crucifix still extended in his hand.

" Are you satisfied now ? " said he.

" That's wanst," said the pilgrim; " you're to touch it three times."

Frank hesitated a moment, but immediately stooped again, and touched it twice in succession; but it remained still and unchanged as before. His father broke the silence by a fervent ejaculation of thanksgiving to God for the vindication of his son's character which he had just witnessed.

" Now ! " exclaimed M'Kenna, in a loud, exulting tone, " you all see that I did not murdher him ! "

" You DID ! " said a voice, which was immediately recognised to be that of the deceased.

M'Kenna shrieked aloud, and immediately fled with his gun towards the mountains, pursued by Reillaghan's other son. The crowd rushed in towards the body, whilst sorrow, affright, and wonder marked the extraordinary scene which ensued.

" Queen o' Heaven ! " exclaimed old M'Kenna, " who could believe this only they hard it ! "

" The murdher wouldn't lie ! " shrieked out Mrs. Reillaghan— " the murdher wouldn't lie !—the blood o' my darlin' son spoke it !—his blood spoke it, or God or His angel spoke it for him ! "

" It's beyant anything ever known," some exclaimed, " to

come back an' tell the deed upon his murdherer! God presarve us an' save us this night! I wish we wor at home out
o' this wild place!"

Others said they had heard of such things; but this, having
happened before their eyes, surpassed anything that could be
conceived.

The mendicant now advanced, and once more mysteriously
held up his crucifix.

"Keep silence!" said he, in a solemn, sonorous voice.
"Keep silence, I say, an' kneel down, all o' yees, before
what I've in my hand. If you want to know who or what
the voice came from, I can tell yees—IT WAS THE CRUCIFIX
THAT SPOKE!"

This communication was received with a feeling of devotion
too deep for words. His injunction was instantly complied
with: they knelt and bent down in worship before it in the
mountain wilds.

"Ay," said he, "little yees know the virtues of that crucifix! It was consecrated by a friar so holy that it was well
known there was but the shadow of him upon the earth, the
other part of him bein' night an' day in heaven among the
archangels. It shows the power of this crass, anyway; an'
you may tell your frinds that I'll sell bades touched wid it
to the faithful at sixpence apiece. They can be put an your
padareens as dicades,[1] wid a blessin'. Oxis Doxis Glorioxis,
Amin! Let us now bear the corpse home, antil it's dressed
an' laid out dacently, as it ought to be."

The body was then placed upon an easy litter, formed of
greatcoats buttoned together, and supported by the strongest
men present, who held it one or two at each corner. In this
manner they advanced at a slow pace until they reached
Owen Reillaghan's house, where they found several of the
country people assembled waiting for their return.

It was not until the body had been placed in an inner
room, where none were admitted until it should be laid out,
that the members of the family first noticed the prolonged
absence of Reillaghan's other son. The moment it had been
alluded to they were seized with new alarm and consternation.

---

[1] Each ten prayers is a "decade."—ED.

"*Hanim an diouol!*" said Reillaghan bitterly, in Irish, "but I doubt the red-handed villain has cut short the lives of two brave sons. I only hope he may stop in the counthry; I'm not widout frinds an' followers that ud think it no sin in a just cause to pay him in his own coin, an' to take from him an' his a pound o' blood for every ounce of ours they shed."

A number of his friends instantly volunteered to retrace their way to the mountains and search for the other son. "There's little danger of his life," said a relation; "it's a short time Frank ud stand him, particularly as the gun wasn't charged. We'll go, at any rate, for fraid he might lose himself in the mountains or walk into some o' the lochs on his way home. We had as good bring some whisky wid us, for he may want it badly."

While they had been speaking, however, the snow began to fall, and the wind to blow in a manner that promised a heavy and violent storm. They proceeded, notwithstanding, on their search, and, on whistling for the dog, discovered that he was not to be found.

"He went wid us to the mountains, I know," said the former speaker; "an' I think it likely he'll be found wid Owen, wherever he is. Come, boys, step out. It's a dismal night, anyway, the Lord knows — och, och!" And with sorrowful but vigorous steps they went in quest of the missing brother.

Nothing but the preternatural character of the words which were so mysteriously pronounced immediately before Owen's pursuit of M'Kenna could have prevented that circumstance, together with the flight of the latter, from exciting greater attention among the crowd. His absence, however, now that they had time to reflect on it, produced unusual alarm, not only on account of M'Kenna's bad character, but from the apprehension of Owen being lost in the mountains.

The inextinguishable determination of revenge with which an Irishman pursues any person who, either directly or indirectly, takes the life of a near relation, or invades the peace of his domestic affections, was strongly illustrated by the nature of Owen's pursuit after M'Kenna, considering the appalling circumstances under which he undertook it. It is certainly more than probable that M'Kenna, instead of flying, would have defended himself with the loaded gun, had not his superstitious fears been excited by the words which so mysteriously charged him with the murder. The direction he accidentally took led both himself and his pursuer into the wildest recesses of the mountains. The chase was close and desperate, and certainly might have been fatal to Reillaghan had M'Kenna thought of using the gun. His terror, however, exhausted him, and overcame his presence of mind to such a degree that, so far from using the weapon in his defence, he threw it aside, in order to gain ground upon his pursuer. This he did but slowly, and the pursuit was as yet uncertain. At length Owen found the distance between himself and his brother's murderer increasing; the night was dark, and he himself feeble and breathless; he therefore gave over all hope of securing him, and returned to follow those who had accompanied him to the spot where his brother's body lay. It was when retracing his path that the nature of his situation occurred to him. The snow had not begun to fall, but the appearance of the sky was strongly calculated to depress him.

Every person knows with what remarkable suddenness snowstorms descend. He had scarcely advanced homewards more than twenty minutes, when the grey tempest spread its dusky wings over the heavens, and a darker shade rapidly settled upon the white hills—now becoming indistinct in the gloom of the air, which was all in commotion, and groaned aloud with the noise of the advancing storm. When he saw the deep gloom, and felt the chilling coldness pierce his flesh so bitterly, he turned himself in the direction which led by the shortest possible cut towards his father's house. He was at this time nearly three miles from any human habitation; and as he looked into the darkness his heart began to palpitate with an alarm almost bordering on hopelessness. His dog, which had, up till this boding change, gone on before him, now partook in his master's apprehensions, and trotted anxiously at his feet.

In the meantime the winds howled in a melancholy manner along the mountains, and carried with them from the upper clouds the rapidly descending sleet. The storm current, too, was against him, and as the air began to work in dark

141

confusion, he felt for the first time how utterly helpless a thing he was under the fierce tempest in this dreadful solitude.

At length the rushing sound which he first heard in the distance approached him in all its terrors; and in a short time he was staggering like a drunken man under the incessant drifts which swept over him and about him. Nothing could exceed the horrors of the atmosphere at this moment. From the surface of the earth the whirlwinds swept immense snow-clouds that rose up instantaneously, and shot off along the brows and ravines of the solitary wild, sometimes descending into the valleys, and again rushing up the almost perpendicular sides of the mountains, with a speed, strength, and noise that mocked at everything possessing life; whilst in the air the tumult and the darkness continued to deepen in the most awful manner. The winds seemed to meet from every point of the compass, and the falling drifts flew backward and forward in every direction; the cold became intense, and Owen's efforts to advance homewards were beginning to fail. He was driven about like an autumn leaf; and his dog, which kept close to him, had nearly equal difficulty in proceeding. No sound but that of the tempest could now be heard, except the screaming of the birds as they were tossed on side-wing through the commotion which prevailed.

In this manner was Owen whirled about, till he lost all know-ledge of his local situation, being ignorant whether he advanced towards home or otherwise. His mouth and eyes were almost filled with driving sleet; sometimes a cloud of light sand-like drift would almost bury him, as it crossed, or followed, or opposed his path; sometimes he would sink to the middle in a snow-wreath, from which he extricated himself with great difficulty; and among the many terrors by which he was beset, that of walking into a lake or over a precipice was not the least paralysing. Owen was a young man of great personal strength and activity, for the possession of which, next to his brother, he had been distinguished among his companions; but he now became totally exhausted: the chase after M'Kenna, his former exertion, his struggles, his repeated falls, his powerful attempts to get into the vicinity of life, the desperate strength he put forth in breaking through the vortex of the whirlwind, all had left him faint and completely at the mercy of the elements.

The cold sleet scales were now frozen to ice on his cheeks; his clothes were completely encrusted with the hard snow which had been beaten into them by the strength of the blast, and his joints were getting stiff and benumbed. The tumult of the tempest, the whirling of the snow-clouds, and the thick snow, now falling, and again tossed upwards by sudden gusts to the sky, deprived him of all power of reflection, and rendered him, though not altogether blind or deaf, yet incapable of forming any distinct opinion upon what he saw or heard. Still, actuated by the unconscious principle of self-preservation, he tottered on, cold, feeble, and breathless, now driven back like a reed by the strong rush of the storm, or prostrated almost to suffocation under the whirlwinds that started up like savage creatures of life about him.

During all this time his faithful dog never abandoned him; but his wild howlings only heightened the horrors of his situation. When he fell, the affectionate creature would catch the flap of his coat, or his arm, in his teeth, and attempt to raise him; and as long as his master had presence of mind, with the unerring certainty of instinct he would turn him, when taking a wrong direction, into that which led homewards.

Owen was not, however, reduced to this state without experiencing sensations of which no language could convey adequate notions. At first he struggled heroically with the storm; but when utter darkness threw its impervious shades over the desolation around him, and the fury of the elements grew so tremendous, all the strong propensities to life became roused, the convulsive throes of a young heart on the steep of death threw a wild and corresponding energy into his vigorous frame, and occasioned him to cling to existence with a tenacity rendered still stronger by the terrible consciousness of his unprepared state, and the horror of being plunged into eternity unsupported by the rites of his Church whilst the crime of attempting to take away human life lay on his soul. Those domestic affections, too, which in Irishmen are so strong, became excited: his home, his fireside, the faces of his kindred, already impressed with affliction for the death of one brother, and the mild countenance of the fair girl to whom he was about to be united, were conjured up in the powerful imagery of natural feeling, the fountains of which were opened in his heart, and his agonising cry for life rose wildly from the mountain desert upon the voice of the tempest. Then, indeed, when the gulf of a twofold death yawned before him, did the struggling spirit send up its shrieking prayer to Heaven with desperate impulse. These struggles, however, as well as those of the body, became gradually weaker as the storm tossed him about, and with the chill of its breath withered him into total helplessness. He reeled on, stiff and insensible, without knowing whither he went, falling with every blast, and possessing scarcely any faculty of life except mere animation.

After about an hour, however, the storm subsided, and the clouds broke away into light fleecy columns before the wind; the air, too, became less cold, and the face of nature more visible. The driving sleet and hard granular snow now ceased to fall, but were succeeded by large feathery flakes that descended slowly upon the still air.

Had this trying scene lasted much longer, Owen must soon have been a stiffened corpse. The child-like strength, however, which just enabled him to bear up without sinking in despair to die, now supported him when there was less demand for energy. The dog, too, by rubbing itself against him and licking his face, enabled him, by a last effort, to recollect himself, so as to have a glimmering perception of his situation. His confidence returned, and with it a greater degree of strength. He shook, as well as he could, the snow from his clothes, where it had accumulated heavily, and felt himself able to proceed, slowly, it is true, towards his father's house, which he had nearly reached when he met his friends, who were once more hurrying out to the mountains in quest of him, having been compelled to return, in consequence of the storm, when they had first set out. The whisky, their companionship, and their assistance soon revived him. One or two were despatched home before them, to apprise the afflicted family of his safety; and the intelligence was hailed with melancholy joy by the Reillaghans. A faint light played

144

for a moment over the gloom which had settled among them, but it was brief; for on ascertaining the safety of their second son, their grief rushed back with renewed violence, and nothing could be heard but the voice of sorrow and affliction.

Darby More, who had assumed the control of the family, did everything in his power to console them; his efforts, however, were viewed with a feeling little short of indignation.

"Darby," said the afflicted mother, "you have, undher God, in some sinse, my fair son's death to account for. You had a dhrame, but you wouldn't tell it to us. If you had, my boy might be livin' this day, for it would be asy for him to be an his guard."

"*Musha,* poor woman!" replied Darby, "sure, you don't know, you afflicted crathur, what you're speakin' about. Tell my dhrame!—why, thin, it's myself tould it to him from beginnin' to ind, and that whin we wor goin' to mass this day itself. I desired him, on the peril of his life, not to go out a-tracin', or toards the mountains, good or bad."

"You said you had a prayer that ud keep it back," observed the mother, "an' why didn't you say it?"

"I did say it," replied Darby, "an' that afore a bit crossed my throath this mornin'; but, you see, he broke his promise of not goin' to the mountains, an' that was what made the dhrame come thrue."

"Well, well, Darby, I beg your pardon, an' God's pardon, for judging you in the wrong. Oh, *wurra sthrue!* my brave son, is it there you're lyin' wid us, *avouneen machree!*" and she again renewed her grief.

"Oh, thin, I'm sure I forgive you," said Darby; "but keep your grief in for a start, till I say the *Deprowhinjis* over him, for the pace an' repose of his sowl. Kneel down, all of yees."

He repeated this prayer in language which it would require one of Edward Irving's adepts in the unknown tongues to interpret. When he had recited about the half of it, Owen and those who had gone to seek him entered the house, and, after the example of the others, reverently knelt down until he finished it.

Owen's appearance once more renewed their grief. The

body of his brother had been removed to a bed beyond the fire in the kitchen; and when Owen looked upon the features of his beloved companion, he approached, and stooped down to kiss his lips. He was still too feeble, however, to bend by his own strength; and it is also probable that the warm air of the house relaxed him. Be this, however, as it may, he fell forward, but supported himself by his hands, which were placed upon the body; a deep groan was heard, and the apparently dead man opened his eyes, and feebly exclaimed, "A dhrink! a dhrink!"

Darby More had, on concluding the *De profundis*, seated himself beside the bed on which Mike lay; but on hearing the groan, and the call for drink, he leaped rapidly to his legs, and exclaimed, "My sowl to hell an' the divil, Owen Reillaghan, but your son's alive! Off wid two or three of yees, as hard as the divil can dhrive yees, for the priest an' docthor!! Off wid yees! Ye damned lazy *spalpeens*, aren't ye near there by this? Give us my cant! Are yees gone? Oh, by this an' by that—hell—eh—aren't yees gone?" but ere he could finish the sentence they had set out.

"Now," he exclaimed, in a voice whose tremendous tones were strongly at variance with his own injunctions—"now, neighbours, d——n yees, keep silence! Mrs. Reillaghan, get a bottle of whisky an' a mug o' wather. Make haste! *Hanim an diouol!* don't be all night!"

The poor mother, however, could not stir; the unexpected revulsion of feeling which she had so suddenly experienced was more than she could sustain. A long fainting fit was the consequence, and Darby's commands were obeyed by the wife of a friendly neighbour.

The mendicant immediately wetted Mike's lips, and poured some spirits, copiously diluted with water, down his throat; after which he held the whisky bottle, like a connoisseur, between himself and the light. "I hope," said he, "this whisky is the ra-al crathur." He put the bottle to his mouth as he spoke, and on holding it a second time before his eye he shook his head complacently. "Ay," said he, "if anything could bring the dead back to this world, my sowl to glory, but that would. Oh, thin, it would give the dead life, sure enough!" He put it once more to his lips, from which

146

it was not separated without relinquishing a considerable portion of its contents.

"*Dhea grasthias!*" he exclaimed; "throth, I find myself the betther o' that sup, in regard that it's good for this touch of configuration that I'm throubled wid inwardly. Oxis Doxis Glorioxis, Amin!" These words he spoke in a low, placid voice, lest the wounded man might be discomposed by his observations.

The rapidity with which the account of Mike's restoration to life spread among the neighbours was surprising. Those who had gone for the priest and doctor communicated it to all they met, and these again to others; so that in a short time the house was surrounded by great numbers of their acquaintances, all anxious to hear the particulars more minutely. Darby, who never omitted an opportunity of impressing the people with a belief in his own sanctity and in that of his crucifix, came out among them and answered their inquiries by a solemn shake of his head and a mysterious indication of his finger to the crucifix, but said nothing more. This was enough. The murmur of reverence and wonder spread among them, and ere long there were few present who did not believe that Reillaghan had been restored to life by a touch of Darby's crucifix; an opinion which is not wholly exploded to this day.

Peggy Gartland, who fortunately had not heard the report of her lover's death until it was contradicted by the account of his revival, now entered, and by her pale countenance betrayed strong symptoms of affection and sympathy. She sat by his side, gazing mournfully on his features, and with difficulty suppressed her tears.

For some time before her arrival the mother and sisters of Mike had been removed to another room, lest the tumultuous expression of their mingled joy and sorrow might disturb him. The fair, artless girl, although satisfied that he still lived, entertained no hopes of his recovery; but she ventured, in a low, trembling voice, to inquire from Darby some particulars of the melancholy transaction which was likely to deprive her of her betrothed husband.

"Where did the shot sthrike him, Darby?"

"Clane through the body, *a villish!* jist where Captain

147

Cramer was shot at the battle o' Bunker's Hill, where he lay as good as dead for twelve hours, an' was near bein' berrid a corp, an' him alive all the time, only that as they were pullin' him off o' the cart he gev a shout, an' thin, *a colleen dhas*, they began to think he might be livin' still. Sure enough, he was too, an' lived successfully, till he died wid dhrinkin' brandy as a cure for the gout—the Lord be praised!"

"Where's the villain, Darby?"

"He's in the mountains, no doubt, where he had thim to fight wid that's a match for him—God, an' the dark storm that fell a while agone. They'll pay him, never fear, for his thrachery to the noble boy that chastised him for your sake, *acushla oge!* Sthrong was your hand, *a veehal*, an' ginerous was your affectionate heart; an' well you loved the fair girl that's sittin' beside you! Throth, Peggy, my heart's black wid sorrow about the darlin' young man. Still, life's in him; an' while there's life there's hope—glory be to God!"

The eulogium of the pilgrim, who was, in truth, much attached to Mike, moved the heart of the affectionate girl, whose love and sympathy were pure as the dew on the grass-blade, and now as easily affected by the slightest touch. She remained silent for a time, but secretly glided her hand towards that of her lover, which she clasped in hers, and by a gentle and timid pressure strove to intimate to him that she was beside him. Long, but unavailing, was the struggle to repress her sorrow: her bosom heaved; she gave two or three loud sobs and burst into tears and lamentations.

"Don't cry, *avourneen*," whispered Darby — "don't cry; I'll warrant you that Darby More will ate share of your weddin' dinner an' his yit. There's a small taste of colour comin' to his face, which, I think, undher God, is owin' to my touchin' him wid the cruciwhix. Don't cry, *a colleen*; he'll get over it, an' more than it, yit, *colleen bann*."

Darby then hurried her into the room where Mike's mother and sisters were. On entering she threw herself into the arms of the former, laid her face on her bosom, and wept bitterly. This renewed the mother's grief; she clasped the interesting girl in a sorrowful embrace; so did his sisters. They threw themselves into each other's arms, and poured

148

forth those touching but wild bursts of pathetic language which are never heard but when the heart is struck by some desolating calamity.

"Husht!" said a neighbouring man who was present; "husht! it's a shame for yees, an' the boy not dead yit."

"I'm not ashamed," said Peggy; "why should I be ashamed of bein' sarry for the likes of Mike Reillaghan? Where was his aquil? Wasn't all hearts upon him? Didn't the very poor on the road bless him whin he passed? Who ever had a bad word agin him but the villain that murdhered him? Murdhered him! Heaven above me! an' why? For my sake! For my sake the pride o' the parish is laid low! Ashamed! Is it for cryin' for my bethrothed husband, that was sworn to me, an' I to him, before the eye of God above us? This day week I was to be his bride; an' now—now ——Oh, Vread [1] Reillaghan, take me to you! Let me go to his mother! My heart's broke, Vread Reillaghan! Let me go to her: nobody's grief for him is like ours. You're his mother, an' I'm his wife in the sight o' God. Proud was I out of him: my eyes brightened when they seen him, an' my heart got light when I heard his voice; an' now what's afore me?—what's afore me but sorrowful days an' a broken heart!"

Mrs. Reillaghan placed her tenderly and affectionately beside her on the bed whereon she herself sat. With the corner of her handkerchief she wiped the tears from the weeping girl, although her own flowed fast. Her daughters also gathered about her, and, in language of the most endearing kind, endeavoured to soothe and console her.

"He may live yet, Peggy, avourneen," said his mother—"my brave an' noble son may live yet, an' you may be both happy. Don't be cryin' so much, asthore galh machree; sure, he's in the hands o' God, avourneen, an' your young heart won't be broke, I hope. Och, the Lord pity her young feelins!" exclaimed the mother, affected even by the consolation she offered to the betrothed bride of her son. "Is it any wondher she'd sink undher sich a blow! for, sure enough, where was the likes of him? No, asthore! it's no

---

[1] Vread is anglicised as Bridget.—ED.

149

wondher—it's no wondher! Lonesome will your heart be widout him; for I know what he'd feel if a hair of your head was injured."

"Oh, I know it—I know it! There was music in his voice, an' *grah* an' kindness to every crathur an God's earth; but to me—to me—oh, no one knew his love to me but myself an' God. Oh, if I was dead, that I couldn't feel this, or if my life could save his! Why didn't the villain—the black villain, wid God's curse upon him—why didn't he shoot me, thin I could never be Mike's wife, an' his hand o' murdher might be satisfied? If he had, I wouldn't feel as I do. Ay, the warmest, an' the best, an' the dearest blood of my heart I could shed for him. That heart was his, an' he had a right to it. Our love wasn't of yisterday: afore the links of my hair came to my showlders I loved him an' thought of him; an' many a time he tould me that I was his first! God knows he was my first, an' he will be my last, let him live or die."

"Well, but Peggy, *achora*," said his sister, "maybe it's sinful to be cryin' this a-way an' he not dead."

"God forgive me, if it's a sin," replied Peggy; "I'd not wish to do anything sinful or displasin' to God; an' I'll sthrive to keep down my grief—I will, as well as I can."

She put her hands on her face, and by an effort of firmness subdued the tone of her grief to a low continuous murmur of sorrow.

"An' along wid that," said the sister, "maybe the noise is disturbin' him. Darby put us all out o' the kitchen, to have pace an' quietness about him."

"An' 'twas well thought o' Darby," she replied, "an' may the blessin' o' God rest upon him for it! A male's mate or a night's lodgin' he'll never want undher my father's roof for that goodness to him. I'll be quiet, thin."

There was now a short pause, during which those in the room heard a smack, accompanied by the words, "*Dhea grasthias!* Throth, I'm the betther o' that sup, so I am. Nothin' keeps this thief of a configuration down but it. *Dhea grasthias* for that! Oh, thin, this *is* the stuff! It warms a body to the tops o' the nails!"

"Don't spare it, Darby," said old Reillaghan, "if it does you good.'

150

"*Avourneen*," said Darby, "it's only what gives me a little relief I ever take, jist by way of cure, for it's the only thing does me good when I'm this a-way."

Several persons in the neighbourhood were, in the meantime, flocking to Reillaghan's house. A worthy man, accompanied by his wife, entered as the pilgrim had concluded. The woman, in accordance with the custom of the country, raised the Irish cry, in a loud, melancholy wail, that might be heard at a great distance.

Darby, who prided himself on maintaining silence, could not preserve the consistency of his character upon this occasion, any more than on that of Mike's recent symptoms of life.

"Your sowl to the divil, you faggot!" he exclaimed; "what do you mane? The divil whip the tongue out o' you, are you goin' to come here only to disturb the boy that's not dead yet? Get out o' this, or be asy wid your skhreechin,' or, by the crass that died for us, only you're a woman, I'd tumble you wid a lick o' my cant. Keep asy, you vagrant, an' the dacent boy not dead yet. Hell bellows you, what do you mane?"

"Not dead!" exclaimed the woman, with her body bent in the proper attitude, her hands extended, and the crying face turned with amazement to Darby—"not dead! *Wurrah,* man alive, isn't he murdhered?"

"Hell resave the matther for that!" replied Darby. "I tell you, he's livin', an' will live, I hope, barrin' your skirlin' dhrives the life that's in him out of him. Go into the room there to the women, an' make yourself scarce out o' this, or, by the *padareens* about me, I'll *malivogue* you."

"We can't be angry wid the dacent woman," observed old Reillaghan, "in regard that she came to show her friendship and respect."

"I'd be angry wid St. Pether," said Darby, "an' ud not scruple to give him a lick o' my c—— Lord presarve us! what was I goin' to say! Why, throth, I believe the little wits I had are all gone *a·shaughran!* I must fast a Friday or two for the same words agin St. Pether. Oxis Doxis Glorioxis, Amin!"

Hope is strong in love and in life. Peggy, now that grief had eased her heart of its load of accumulated sorrow, began to reflect upon Darby's anecdote of Captain Cramer, which she related to those about her. They all rejoiced to hear that it was possible to be wounded so severely and live. They also consoled and supported each other, and expressed their trust that Mike might also recover. The opinion of the doctor was waited for with such anxiety as a felon feels when the foreman of the jury hands down the verdict which consigns him to life or death.

Whether Darby's prescription was the result of chance or sagacity we know not. We are bound, however, to declare that Reillaghan's strength was in some degree restored, although the pain he suffered amounted to torture. The surgeon (who was also a physician, and, moreover, supplied his own medicines) and the priest, as they lived in the same town, both arrived together. The latter administered the rites of his Church to him ; and the former, who was a skilful man, left nothing undone to accomplish his restoration to health. He had been shot through the body with a bullet—a circumstance which was not known until the arrival of the surgeon. This gentleman expressed much astonishment at his surviving the wound, but said that circumstances of a similar nature had occurred, particularly on the field of battle, although he admitted that they were few.

Darby, however, who resolved to have something like a decided opinion from him, without at all considering whether such a thing was possible, pressed him strongly upon the point.

" *Arrah,* blur-an-ager, Docthor Swither, say one thing or other—is he to live or die ? Plain talk, docthor, is all we want, an' no *feasthalagh.*"

" The bullet, I am inclined to think," replied the doctor, " must either not have touched a vital part, or touched it only slightly. I have known cases similar, it is true ; but it is impossible for me to pronounce a decisive opinion upon him just now."

" The divil resave the yarrib [1] ever I'll gather for you agin, so long as my name's Darby More, except you say either 'life' or 'death,'" said Darby, who forgot his character of sanctity altogether.

[1] Herb.

"Darby, *achora*," said Mrs. Reillaghan, "don't crass the gintleman, an' him sthrivin' to do his best. Here, Paddhy Gormly, bring some wather till the docthor washes his hands."

"Darby," replied the doctor, to whom he was well known, "you are a good herbalist, but even although you should not serve me as usual in that capacity, yet I cannot say exactly either life or death; the case is too critical a one; but I do not despair, Darby, if that will satisfy you."

"More power to you, docthor, *achora*. Hell-an-age, where's that bottle?—bring it here. Thank you, Vread. Docthor, here's wishin' you all happiness, an' may you set Mike on his legs wanst more ! See, docthor—see, man alive—look at this purty girl here, wid her wet cheeks; give her some hope, *ahagur*, if you can; keep the crathur's spirits up, an' I'll furnish you wid every yarrib in Europe, from the nettle to the rose."

"Don't despair, my good girl," said the doctor, addressing Peggy; "I hope—I trust that he may recover, but he must be kept easy and quiet."

"May the blessin of God, sir, light down on you for the same words," replied Peggy, in a voice tremulous with gratitude and joy.

"Are you done wid him, docthor ?" said old Reillaghan.

"At present," replied the doctor, "I can do nothing more for him; but I shall see him early to-morrow morning."

"Bekase, sir," continued the worthy man, "here's Darby More, who's afflicted wid a conflamboration, or some sich thing, inwardly, an' if you could ase him, sir, I'd pay the damages, whatever they might be."

The doctor smiled slightly. "Darby's complaint," said he, "is beyond my practice; there is but one cure for it, and that is, if I have any skill, a little of what's in the bottle here, taken, as our prescriptions sometimes say, 'when the patient is inclined for it.' "

"By my sou—sanctity, docthor," said Darby, "you're a man o' skill, anyhow, an' that's well known, sir. Nothin', as Father Hoolaghan says, but the sup o' whisky does this sarra of a configuration good. It rises the wind off o' my stomach, docthor."

153

"It does, Darby, it does. Now let all be peace and quietness," continued the doctor. "Take away a great part of this fire, and don't attempt to remove him to any other bed until I desire you. I shall call again to-morrow morning, early."

The doctor's attention to his patient was unremitting; everything that human skill, joined to long experience and natural talent, could do to restore the young man to his family was done; and in the course of a few weeks the friends of Reillaghan had the satisfaction of seeing him completely out of danger.

Mike declared, after his recovery, that, though incapable of motion on the mountains, he was not altogether insensible to what passed around him. The loud tones of their conversation he could hear. The oath which young M'Kenna uttered in a voice so wild and exalted, fell clearly on his ear, and he endeavoured to contradict it, in order that he might be secured and punished in the event of his death. He also said that the pain he suffered in the act of being conveyed home occasioned him to groan feebly, but that the sobs, and cries, and loud conversation of those who surrounded him prevented his moans from being heard. It is probable, after all, that were it not for the accidental fall of Owen upon his body he might not have survived the wound, inasmuch as the medical skill which contributed to restore him would not have been called in.

Though old Frank M'Kenna and his family felt an oppressive load of misery taken off their hearts by the prospect of Reillaghan's recovery, yet it was impossible for them to be insensible to the fate of their son, knowing, as they did, that he must have been out among the mountains during the storm. His unhappy mother and Rody sat up the whole night, expecting his return, but morning arrived without bringing him home. For six days afterwards the search for him was general and strict: his friends and neighbours traversed the mountain wastes until they left scarcely an acre of them unexplored. On the sixth day there came a thaw, and towards the close of the seventh he was found a " stiffened corpse," UPON THE VERY SPOT WHERE HE HAD SHOT HIS RIVAL, and on which he had challenged the Almighty to stretch him in death, without priest or prayer, if he were guilty

154

of the crime with which he had been charged. He was found lying with a circle drawn round him, his head pillowed upon the innocent blood which he had shed with the intention of murder, and a bloody cross marked upon his breast and forehead. It was thought that in the dread of approaching death he had formed it with his hand, which came accidentally in contact with the blood that lay in clots about him.

The manner of his death excited a profound and wholesome feeling among the people with respect to the crime which he attempted to commit. The circumstances attending it, and his oath upon the spot where he shot Reillaghan, are still spoken of by the fathers of the neighbouring villages, and even by some who were present at the search for his body. It was also doubly remarkable on account of a case of spectral illusion which it produced, and which was ascribed to the effect of M'Kenna's supernatural appearance at the time. The daughter of a herdsman in the mountains was strongly affected by the spectacle of his dead body borne past her father's door. In about a fortnight afterwards she assured her family that he appeared to her. She saw the apparition, in the beginning, only at night; but ere long it ventured, as she imagined, to appear in daylight. Many imaginary conversations took place between them; and the fact of the peasantry flocking to the herd's house, to satisfy themselves as to the truth of the rumour, is yet well remembered in the parish. It was also affirmed that as the funeral of M'Kenna passed to the churchyard a hare crossed it, which some one present struck on the side with a stone. The hare, says the tradition, was not injured, but the sound of the stroke resembled that produced on striking an empty barrel.

We have nearly wound up our story, in which we have feebly endeavoured to illustrate scenes that were, some time ago, not unusual in Irish life. There is little more to be added, except that Mike Reillaghan almost miraculously recovered, that he and Peggy Gartland were happily married, and that Darby More lost his character as a dreamer in that part of the parish. Mike, with whom, however, he still continued a favourite, used frequently to allude to the speaking crucifix, the dream aforesaid, and his bit of fiction in assuring his mother that he had dissuaded him against "tracing" on that eventful day.

"Well, *avourneen*," Darby would exclaim, "the holiest of us has our failins; but, in throth, the truth of it is that myself didn't know what I was sayin', I was so through other,[1] for I remimber that I was badly afflicted wid this thief of a configuration inwardly at the time. That, you see, an' your own throubles, put my mind *a shaughran* for a start. But, upon my sanctity—an', sure, that's a great oath wid me—only for the holy carol you bought from me the night before, an', above all, touchin' you wid the blessed crucifix, you'd never ha' got over the same accident. Oh, you may smile an' shake your head, but it's thruth whether or not! Glory be to God!"

The priest of the parish, on ascertaining correctly the incidents mentioned in this sketch, determined to deprive the people of at least one pretext for their licentiousness. He represented the abuses connected with such a ceremony to the bishop; and from that night to the present time the inhabitants of Kilnaheery never had, in their own parish, an opportunity of hearing a Midnight Mass.

[1] Agitated.

156